Life Goes On

Another Vantage Press title by this author:

Let Us Live (2004)

Life Goes On

Michael P. Verticchio

VANTAGE PRESS
New York

This is a work of fiction. Any similarity between the names
and characters in this book and any real persons, living
or dead, is purely coincidental.

FIRST EDITION

Published by Vantage Press, Inc.
419 Park Ave. South, New York, NY 10016

Manufactured in the United States of America
ISBN: 0-533-15331-X

Library of Congress Catalog Card No.: 2005907565

0 9 8 7 6 5 4 3 2 1

I dedicate this book, *Life Goes On*, to my two brothers, Paul and Marion.

All three Verticchio brothers attended a country school and taught in a country school.

Paul, the oldest, only taught two years, then graduated from law school, and went into law practice in Benld, Gillespie, and Macoupin County, Illinois.

Paul was elected State's Attorney of Macoupin County for two terms and then was elected Judge of the Seventh Judicial Circuit of Illinois for the counties of Greene, Jersey, Macoupin, Morgan, Sangamon, and Scott until he retired.

Marion spent a lifetime in education. After starting his teaching in a country school, he went to the Livingston, Illinois High School and taught science and mathematics. He became principal of the Livingston High School and Superintendent of the Livingston Community Unit in Madison County until he retired.

Acknowledgment

I want to thank Lou Ann Brown, retired art teacher of Southwestern School District in Macoupin County, Illinois, for the sketch on the front cover of my book, *Life Goes On.*

Introduction

My first book, *Let Us Live,* tells the story of Mary Belle and Marion Victori, immigrants from Italy who meet on a boat coming to the United States in the early 20th century.

Mary Belle is on her way to the bituminous coal mining region of Illinois where her sister's husband is a coal miner in the Old Maggie Mine in Kollinson. Marion goes to New York City first, but does not like the city and soon follows Mary to Kollinson. Marion gets a job in the Old Maggie Mine, renews acquaintance with Mary Belle, and they get married. The couple has four children: Tommy, the oldest; twins, Paul and Jimmy; and a daughter, Kay.

Both Mary Belle and Marion go to night school to study to become American citizens.

After fifteen years as a hand loader and motorman, Marion develops a cough from the bituminous coal. The family moves to Hinders where a new coal mine is sunk. Marion builds a frame house with a store front, hoping to make a living in business and quit the mine when the store is a success.

When there is a long coal strike, Hinders, the mine owner, brings in Negroes to break the strike. When the angered miners take action, Marion Victori is killed by the guards in the shootout.

The Victori store fails during the long strike. Mary Victori turns to bootlegging during prohibition.

Hinders sells the mine to the John Sampson Coal Company. The strike ends, and Mary Victori's store becomes a success.

Hinders is a typical Illinois coal mining village, where the miners and their families struggle through strikes and hardships, but manage to live a life that makes them proud to be Americans.

The story ends as Tommy Victori graduates from high school and enrolls in college.

Life Goes On

One

Tommy Victori decided to look for work at one of the four Superior Coal Mines around Gilmore. He didn't want to go to the bottom and shovel coal. His friends, Harry and Tony, offered to take him as a partner, but Tommy intended to attend Illinois College in Jacksonville in the fall. He had already applied and been accepted, so all he wanted was a summer job.

At the superintendent's office he explained to Mr. Powers that he would like to learn surveying, since he was interested in becoming a mathematician. Mr. Powers was a personable gentleman who was interested in helping a widow's son. Thus, Tommy was hired as a surveyor's assistant. He would spend a good deal of his time at the bottom of the mine but also be doing diagrams and blue prints in the surveyor's office in a building adjoining the mine.

When Tommy went home that evening and told his mother about the job and how he would be paid five dollars a day, Mary was overjoyed and gave an extra prayer thanking God for their good fortune.

After supper, Tommy knocked on Ann's door. Ann came to the door with a big smile when she saw Tommy. Ann said, "Come in."

Tommy said, "Ann, I have something important to tell you. Can you go for a walk?"

Ann looked at Tommy askance before saying, "I'll be out in a couple of minutes."

Tommy sat on the porch swing waiting for Ann. As soon as she came out of the door, Tommy got up from the swing. He grabbed Ann's hand and hurried down the porch steps.

"Ann, I have a summer job as a surveyor's helper with the Superior Mines."

"Gee, Tommy that's wonderful," cried Ann. "As you know, I'll be working full time at Woolworth's. I'll be making two dollars a day."

Tommy hesitated, and then decided he would not tell Ann what his wages were.

"By the way, Tommy, I have been accepted at Carmount College. The room, board, and tuition is two hundred dollars a year. Of course, they have a work program, and I'll work fifteen hours a week at the college."

"Ann, the tuition at Illinois College is two hundred dollars a year and I'll have to find a job for my room and board."

"Tommy, why don't you go to Carmount? It'll be cheaper and we'll be going to school together?"

"Ann, I'm sorry, but I've already enrolled at Illinois College. If it doesn't work out, I'll transfer to Carmount next year. But, as you know, Carmount is only a two year college, and I will have to transfer at the end of my sophomore year anyway."

"Tommy, let's enjoy our summer. We'll worry about college this fall."

"You're right, Ann," said Tommy as he put his arm around her, pulled her to him, and kissed her cheek. Ann laughed as they climbed Hinders Hill.

As they overlooked Hinders Pond, Tommy said, "I'm not going to suggest that we go swimming tonight after what happened as we left Hamburg's in June."

They both let out a loud scream as they remembered their swim to the raft on that June night.

Two

Tommy climbed into the mine cage with the surveyor, John Combs. John looked at Tommy as he followed Combs's lead and grabbed the hook above his head as the cage began to drop. "Just hang on, Tommy. The first trip is always a little frightening, but after a few trips you'll get used to the three-hundred-foot travel straight down."

Tommy could feel a sinking sensation in his stomach as he sped downward. His miner's lamp fluttered as they traveled. It seemed he has just started to brace himself as the cage began to slow down and came to a halt.

"Here's where we get off," said Combs. Tommy followed the surveyor and walked to where a motor was waiting for him. "Yes, we have good communication from the top to the bottom, so we can get things done," said Mr. Combs.

"We are going to the south end of the mine where we are extending an entry, and I'll do a little surveying."

As they reached their destination, Combs took out his transit, a small telescope set up on a tripod.

"Tommy, I'm going to show you how to use this transit. Within a week, you'll be able to do a little surveying and by the time the summer is over, you'll be a surveyor. Well, almost."

Tommy came home after his first day on the job as surveyor's helper. As he entered the back door to the kitchen his mother, Kay, and the twins hollered, "Surprise!" and started to clap their hands.

Paul said, "We been waiting for you."

Jimmy screamed, "It's about time you got home. What did you do? Take half an hour in the miners wash-house shower?"

Kay said, "Don't pay attention to him. We are really proud of you."

Mary laughed. She put her arms around Tommy and said a prayer, "God, our Heavenly Father, we thank You for Your kindness and please remember us to their father as You bless this food to our health."

Three

It was the Fourth of July. Tommy and Ann, his mother, the twins, and Kay were going to Gilmore to the carnival and then planned to stay for the fireworks at ten P.M.

They had traded in their Model T truck for a Model T 1926 four-door touring car, which had windows instead of curtains.

As they reached the carnival and parked, Mary said, "Kay and I will stay together, the twins and Tommy and Ann will want to go their own way. At ten o'clock, we'll meet here in the parking lot to watch the fireworks and then we'll all head for home, okay?"

They all shouted, "Okay."

Tommy and Ann said, "We'll just walk around to see the carnival."

Jimmy said, "I think Paul and I will just follow Ann and Tommy and see where they go."

Paul said, "Cut it out, Jimmy. You know we are heading for the Ferris wheel."

Mary said, "Kay and I are starting with the craft show."

After the Ferris wheel, Jimmy and Paul decided to walk around. When they came to the boxing show, they decided to watch and listen.

A barker came out on a platform with two boxers. He shouted, "I have two boxers here, one is a middle weight and he will challenge anyone in the audience up to two hundred pounds to stay three rounds with him. The other is a heavy weight, and he will challenge anyone

5

at any weight to stay with him for three rounds. Any challenger that stays three rounds with either fighter will received one hundred dollars. Admission is one dollar for both shows. That's right. You get to watch both shows for one dollar."

Jimmy and Paul decided to see the show. They waited in the tent for one-half hour before two challengers and two carnival boxers, all in boxing trunks, came into the tent. The barker handed each boxer a pair of gloves. Then he brought the middle weights to the center of the ring. He spoke to the two middle weights, and they went to two opposite corners.

The barker faced the audience, who was getting impatient. There were about 200 people in the tent. The barker held up a hand. He pointed to the challenger and said, "The challenger is Frank House from Gilmore. He is six feet tall and weighs," the challenger jumped on the scale, "one hundred ninety-eight pounds. His opponent is a carnival boxer, Sam Mann, who is six feet tall and weighs," the carnival boxer got on the scale, "one hundred ninety-six pounds."

The barker sent the fighters to their corners and said, "I want to introduce the referee. He is the chief of police of Gilmore, Joe Josepi."

The referee brought the fighters to the center of the ring, had them touch gloves, and then blew a whistle to start the fight. The boxers circled each other for ten seconds, and then the carnival man threw a left, then a right. The challenger stepped back to avoid the force of the blows to the head. Then he delivered a right to the midsection that made the carnival boxer flinch. This brought the crowd to its feet, shouting for the Gilmore challenger.

The fight continued as they exchanged rights and lefts. The first round lasted for three minutes. Jimmy and Paul really got excited and joined the crowd to root for Frank House of Gilmore.

After a minute between rounds, the referee's whistle, which had started and ended the first round, sounded to start the second round. Again, they exchanged rights and lefts to the head. Then they went into a clinch, and the referee separated them. As Frank House let his arms down after the referee parted them, Sam Mann stepped forward so rapidly that Frank House was caught unprepared and took a right and a left to the chin and went down and lay on the canvas. The chief of police, the referee, stood over Frank and counted slowly to ten. Then he raised Sam Mann's right hand and announced Sam Mann as the winner.

Jimmy and Paul had never seen a boxing match before and couldn't believe that the fight was over. The barker grabbed a horn and shouted to the crowd. "The champion heavy weight fight starts in two minutes. The heavy weight is Jack Quick from Sawyer, six feet two inches tall and weighs in," Jack got on the scale, "at two hundred-fifty pounds. Now the carnival man, Joe White, who is six feet tall and weighs in," Joe White got on the scale, "at two hundred twenty-five pounds."

The chief of police brought the two fighters to the center of the ring. They touched gloves. The referee blew his whistle, and the two big men started to pound each other, left and rights to the face, followed by body blows until the round ended with a whistle.

Jimmy and Paul couldn't believe that both men were still standing. The boys didn't realize that the fighters wore padded gloves.

The fighting went on for two more rounds. Jack Quick of Sawyer had a bloody nose, but he was still standing at the end of three rounds. The crowd shouted and cheered as Jack Quick was presented with a hundred-dollar bill.

Mary and Kay spent over half an hour at the craft show. Then they both got on a horse on the merry-go-round, and laughed and laughed as they went up and down and around on the horses.

Tommy and Ann rode the Ferris wheel, and then walked around the carnival hand in hand.

They all had a hot dog and Coke, and then they all met at the band stand to listen to the music. At ten o'clock, they were all in the parking lot near their car to watch the fireworks. They saw rockets of all colors for an hour. The grand finale was the American flag with red, white, and blue and the playing of the National Anthem.

Tommy dropped his mother, the twins, and Kay off at home and said, "Good night!"

Just as soon as they were alone Ann slid close to Tommy. Tommy said, "Alone at last. Where do we go now?"

Ann said, "It can't be very far. It will soon be midnight. Let's settle for my porch. It's nice and airy there. This July weather is hot and humid."

"I'll have to tell Mom so she'll know I'm home and on our porch," said Ann.

Tommy headed for the swing. A few minutes later Ann joined him.

"Mom told me she expected me in the house in fifteen minutes," said Ann.

"That doesn't leave much time for hugs and kisses," said Tommy.

Ann sat on Tommy's lap, kissed him, and laughed. "Don't worry, Tommy. We'll have the rest of our lives for loving."

Four

John Combs was right. By the end of the week, Tommy found riding up and down the cage routine. Sure enough, Friday, the last day of the week, Combs handed Tommy the transit and tripod. He said, "Tommy I want you to measure a few angles, using the vernier to get them exact, Then, using the telescope, I want you to determine several distances. You'll use the one-hundred-foot tape to check your calculations.

"Tommy, the basis of surveying is geometry. Angles and triangles play a very important part in the work. Surveyors must have a thorough knowledge of geometry and trigonometry. They must be able to use delicate instruments with precision and accuracy."

Tommy felt lucky to be working with John Combs, an experienced and knowledgeable surveyor who had the patience to teach a beginner. In the office near the mine, where the drawings and blue prints were put together, Tommy was happy he had taken a course in mechanical drawing in high school, where he learned to use triangles, T-squares, and drafting tables.

In the drafting rooms Tommy saw drafting machines that combined several drawing tools, a protractor, scale, T-square, and triangle. The device helped draft work quickly and efficiently. Tommy realized he had a lot to learn, but he was genuinely interested and was willing to listen to his teacher, Mr. Combs.

Five

The summer went by quickly, and Tommy found himself in their Ford with his mother, the twins, and Kay on their way to Jacksonville, headed for Illinois College. Tommy was driving.

"Mom, you can drive back to Hinders. I know it is only sixty miles, and the twins want to drive back, but they aren't old enough to be driving."

The twins gave a big Bronx cheer as they laughed at Tommy. Jimmy said, "You won't be with us on the way home, and we are better drivers than Mom."

Tommy had paid a month's rent to the school for room and board. He wanted to have a place to stay while he looked for places to work for his meals and for an old man and woman who had an extra room where he could stay. In return, he could cut the grass and take care of the furnace.

Tommy took his mother, the twins, and Kay to the visitors' room in the dorm. Then one of the seniors in charge of the dorms shouted, "Woman on board" as he lead the family to the second floor. They all met in Tommy's room where he met his freshman roommate, a young man from Springfield.

When it was time for the family to leave, Mary put her arms around Tommy, kissed him, and said, "We'll see you in Hinders in a couple of weeks. I'm sure you'll have a lot to tell us."

Kay kissed Tommy and began to cry. "Tommy, we'll sure miss you."

The twins shook hands with Tommy and said in unison, "We'll miss you, big brother."

On the way home, Mary drove, and everyone was very quiet. Mary's thoughts were not only of Tommy, whose separation from his family was only temporary, but of the sad, sad night nearly four years ago when Marion was killed in the strike and left them forever.

After one-half-hour of travel, Jimmy punched Paul in the ribs, made a forced laugh and loudly said, "Come on, now, Tommy is in college. This is not a wake. Let's stop at the Candy Kitchen in Carmount and have a soda."

They all agreed, but even after they had the soda, when they entered their home in Hinders without Tommy, they put their arms around each other and all cried together.

Six

Tommy registered for classes in chemistry, algebra, German, and English. It didn't take him long to get in the school routine.

Tommy would never forget his second night at the college dormitory. It was about ten o'clock and Tommy was getting ready for bed when the upper classmen in the dorm began screaming, "All freshmen rooming in the dorm meet in the lounge for a prayer meeting wearing only shorts."

Some of the freshman tried to stay in their room. The upper classmen had all the freshmen names and went to each room to collar the freshmen. They said, "If you don't attend the prayer meeting tonight, we'll get you later this week and you'll be sorry."

There were about twelve freshmen and twenty-five upper classmen at the meeting. Two of the seniors said, "We want you to sing. We'll help you with the song." One of the upper classmen sat at the piano and began to play "America." The upper classmen sang louder than the freshmen.

"Not bad," said the two leaders.

One of the leaders stepped forward and called a freshman by name. The freshman stepped forward. The senior who called his name said, "Each freshman will receive a whack from this paddle if you do not answer a question correctly. We'll give each freshman a number. You are number one." The senior put a tag on the freshman with a #1.

Question: "Do you masturbate?"

The freshman refused to answer.

"Bend over."

The freshman bent over and received a whack. Everybody laughed except the freshman. One of the seniors called another name. The freshman was given the number two.

Question: "Do you masturbate?"

The freshman answered. "Never."

"You get a whack for lying."

Again there was laughter and screaming from the upper classmen. Tommy's name was called and given the number three.

Question: "Do you masturbate?"

Tommy said, "All boys do."

The senior said, "You did not answer the question. Bend over."

Tommy received a whack, which had a sting to it.

All twelve freshmen were asked the same question and given a whack with the paddle. Then the two seniors in charge said, "Congratulations. You all passed your first prayer meeting. You are dismissed."

Tommy made several trips to the student employment office looking for work for his meals and a room. He was hired by Joe Moore, the owner of Moore's Café, to work two hours a day, an hour per meal. He decided to skip breakfast and spend the hours each evening waiting tables. The café was near the square and about a mile from Illinois College. He only wanted to walk uptown two times a day, once for lunch and once when he went to Moore's to work in the evening.

At the end of the first week, Tommy was still looking for a room. Then he got a call from the employment office stating that the Gill Funeral Home had a room for a college kid who would be willing to fire the stoker and take out the ash clinkers. Tommy decided to check it out.

Mr. Gill interviewed Tommy and showed him the upstairs room which had a bed, a desk, and an adjoining bathroom. He told Tommy that clean bed sheets and towels would be furnished each week, but Tommy would have to keep his room clean and make his own bed. Mr. Gill had another surprise for Tommy when he said that the funeral home would pay $3.50 a week, cash.

After the interview, Tommy was hired and Mr. Gill said they would send a truck to Illinois College dormitory to move his belongings.

Tommy moved in that weekend. Tommy learned that the funeral homes in Jacksonville took turns taking care of bodies from the State Mental Hospital, and Gill had September. The first weekend he was left alone, when all the grieving relatives and the funeral personnel left, with five bodies, three whites and two blacks.

Tommy did not believe in ghosts, but when he was left alone, he hesitated going to bed upstairs with the five bodies downstairs. The only time he remembered being in a house with a dead person was when his father's wake was held in their home in Hinders. He told himself he was not afraid but it was after midnight before he fell into a troubled sleep. During the night, when he had to go to the bathroom, he was glad his bathroom adjoined his room and he didn't have to go downstairs where the bodies were.

When Tommy told his mother about his job at the funeral home and the dead bodies, Mary said, "Never fear the dead. They will never harm you. However, keep your cyoo opon for the living. Most people are trustworthy, but there are those who would take advantage of you."

Seven

Instead of two weeks, it was a month before Tommy hitchhiked home to Hinders on the fourth weekend after starting college.

His mother, the twins, Kay, and Ann were waiting for him that Saturday afternoon. The family and Ann all hugged him. Mary said, "I'm preparing a special supper tonight for Tommy and the family. Ann, you are welcome to come."

Ann said, "Thank you, Mrs. Victori. I'll be here. However, I'm going home now so the family can be together and catch up on news of the last month."

Tommy walked through the four rooms of the living quarters and then slowly through what was now a well-stocked country store. He turned to his mother and asked, "How are things going, Mother?"

Mary said, "Very well, Tommy, but we really miss you."

Tommy said, "I sure miss all of you, but I'm sure none of us would want it any other way."

At supper that evening, they talked and talked and praised Mary's spaghetti and meatballs, Italian salad, and her blackberry pie and pizzelles.

That evening Tommy and Ann went to Hamburg's. They met their old friends Louis Looke, Sally Sponich, Dean Basse, Mary Bruno, Tony Prima, and Harry Shinski. They danced the evening away. Tommy and Ann had a wonderful time. Their friends couldn't get enough dances with Tommy and Ann, the only ones who were away in college.

After the dance, Tommy and Ann walked to Tommy's house, got into the Victoris' Ford, and headed for the Gilmore Lake. They parked near the dam. It was a clear night and they could see the water glistening in the moonlight as it rushed over the dam.

Ann was in Tommy's arms and was first to utter a word. She looked up at Tommy and said, "How is school going?" She had received several letters from Tommy complaining about his room arrangement.

Tommy said, "I'm getting used to the funeral home, but I'll never become a funeral director. The classes are going nicely and I'm getting acquainted. What about you?"

Ann replied, "I'm enjoying myself and my classes are okay. As for my work, I've been assigned to the women's dean's office. When they learned I was a good typist and could take shorthand, they had no trouble placing me."

Tommy said, "It was sure a treat talking to and dancing with our old friends at Hamburg's. Have you gone to any dances at Carmount College?"

Ann said, "No, Tommy. I've been waiting to talk to you. Tommy, do you think it would be alright to go to the college dances?"

Tommy said, "I love you dearly, Ann, and nobody could ever take your place. However, we should probably go to a few school dances if for no other reason than to show that no one could interfere in our love."

Ann said, "I think you are right. Tommy, let's give it a try and see."

When Tommy dropped Ann off at her home a little later, he hugged her more closely and kissed her for a longer period than ever before.

Eight

Two years passed. Tommy had finished his second year in college, and Ann was graduating from Carmount. She had majored in education, and her student teaching completed, she took an elementary teaching position at Gilmore.

Tommy was getting ready to go back to his summer job in surveying. However, tonight was a special night. Ann was graduating from Carmount's two year college.

Tommy, Mary, the twins, and Kay were all invited and were all going to Ann's graduation in their Model T. They were all in good spirits as they traveled to Carmount gym where the graduation was being held.

"Don't forget," said Tommy. "I'm taking all of you, Ann, Harry, and Mr. and Mrs. Shinski, out to the Gardens for dinner after graduation. Harry is going to see that the Shinskis get there."

Tommy and Harry had their cameras with them and insisted on group pictures: the Shinskis, the whole group, with the assistance of the waitress, and pictures of Ann with her parents, Harry and Ann, and Tommy and Ann.

They had all clapped and called Ann's name when the president of the college awarded Ann her diploma. Ann had finished in the upper ten percent of the fifty graduates.

Mr. Shinski gave grace, thanking God for being so good to them. Tommy, sitting near Ann, smiled at her and said, "You really looked good in your cap and gown."

Ann said, "Thank you, Tommy, but every parent, girlfriend, and boyfriend felt the same way."

Tommy said, "Ann, you are probably right. Beauty is in the eyes of the beholder."

After the dinner, Ann went home with Harry and her parents. Tommy drove the Victoris home.

As they approached the railroad crossing at Hinders, Jimmy said, "Don't tell us that you are going home with us?"

Paul said, "That would be the day."

Tommy said, "You guys are right for once. The Shinskis have invited me over to their house."

Jimmy laughed, "They want to keep an eye on you."

Kay scolded the twins, "Can't you guys quit picking on Tommy?"

Mary said, "I agree with her. Jimmy and Paul, cut it out."

Tommy did go to the Victori home and changed to slacks and a sport shirt. Then he told them all good night and walked out of the door on his way to Ann's house.

When Tommy knocked on the door and walked into the Shinskis' living room, Mr. Shinski went to the cellar and came back with a bottle of his prized wine and five glasses. Mr. Shinski poured out the wine, and his wife brought each one a glass and a napkin. They all waited until everyone was served, and Mr. Shinski said, "I want to give a toast. To my wonderful daughter, Ann. May she be a good teacher and always as happy as she is tonight."

After a couple of glasses of wine, Tommy said, "I want to thank you for inviting me over. You all know what I think of Ann, but I'm leaving so the Shinski family can enjoy a little time together."

Ann rose and said, "I'll walk with you to the end of the block, Tommy."

When they were alone, Tommy put his arm around Ann as they walked and said, "I can't wait until I graduate, get a job, and buy you a ring."

Ann replied, "I'm looking forward to that day, Tommy." And he kissed her good night.

Nine

Tommy got up at six o'clock every morning and was at the mine before seven taking the cage to the bottom. Mary had his breakfast, bacon and eggs over hard, toast, orange juice, and coffee, ready and hurried him along. Tommy always thanked his mother and gave her a hug. Tommy, six feet tall and now one hundred eighty pounds, reminded Mary more and more of Marion every year.

Tommy had talked to Harry and Tony at the dance and found out that they were working near where he and Mr. Combs were surveying. After Mr. Combs and he completed their surveying and put their tools on the motor that would take them to the next location, Tommy told Mr. Combs he would like to spend a few minutes visiting Tony and Harry and watching them work. John Combs said, "We are way ahead of schedule. Let's go."

They stopped near the entry where Tony and Harry were working. They watched Harry and Tony shoveling coal for at least five minutes. Tony and Harry did it so easily that it looked effortless. They never got in the other fellow's way. When Tony and Harry saw Tommy and Combs, they stopped.

Harry said, "Me and Tony have worked together for years and you are the first people that have come to watch us work. The bosses and other miners have seen us shovel coal, but you two are the only ones that ever came as an audience."

Tommy introduced Mr. Combs to his friends and said, "Mr. Combs is a top notch surveyor and a darn good teacher. This is the third summer I have worked for him. I have enjoyed it, and I have learned a lot."

Mr. Combs said, "Hold it, Tommy, and give some of the credit to the student who was willing and able to learn."

After a few minutes, Mr. Combs and Tommy were walking back to their motor when they heard an emergency whistle. They pulled over to a side track and waited to see what the problem was. They were ready to head for their next surveying location when the mine whistle indicated that the mine was shutting down for the day.

Mr. Combs, who had spent many years in the coal mines, said to Tommy, "I'm afraid there has been a serious accident for the mine to blow off with hours to go on the day shift."

When they took the cage to the surface, they found out the roof had fallen in on two miners, killing one and seriously injuring the other man who had been taken to the Carmount hospital.

Mr. Combs told Tommy, "This is the worst accident we have had here since we dug into the old Tom Mine in the early twenties and lost five miners."

Ten

Tommy started his junior year at Illinois College. After a discussion with his mother he decided to concentrate on his school work and stay in the college dorm and eat in the school cafeteria. After a discussion with his school counselor, he decided to continue to major in physical science and math. But of all the things, get a minor in education, because he was considering teaching chemistry and physics and going to Lincoln Law School at night in Springfield.

Ann started teaching at Gilmore for a yearly salary of seven hundred twenty dollars, sixty dollars a month for twelve months. The miners at the Hinders mine were getting five dollars a day, twenty-five dollars a week, but they worked very little during the summer. Then, too, Ann had worked summers at Woolworth's for two dollars a day, so she felt good about her teaching position in the Gilmore School.

That weekend Tommy's roommate persuaded him to go to the school opening dance. Although Tommy and Ann had agreed that they should go to the college dances, Tommy had never gone. Ann had never mentioned going to college dances, and Tommy had never asked.

Tommy's roommate was a junior from Springfield. They went to the dance, and Tommy stood around while John Vana, his roommate, danced every dance. Finally, John brought a girlfriend's friend over and introduced her to Tommy as Jane Miller. Jane was also a junior at Illinois College. Tommy had to admit to himself that she was not bad to look at. Jane was about five-feet-seven-inches tall with dark brown hair and dark brown eyes. They waltzed well together. Tommy thanked Jane and went back to standing along the wall. Later he asked Jane for another dance. After the dance, John asked him and Jane to go out to a night spot with him and his girlfriend, Sarah. Tommy felt trapped, but said, "Yes."

John was one of the few students who had a car at the college. They rode in John's old Dodge a mile out of Jacksonville. Tommy realized that liquor was still illegal in 1926, but that part did not bother him. However, he felt that he was not being true to Ann. Everybody was jovial and talking and Tommy joined in not wanting to be a stick in the mud.

After a couple or glasses of wine, John took the girls to their dorm, and he and Tommy went back to the boys' dormitory.

Eleven

When John and Tommy returned to their room, Tommy explained that the picture of Ann was more than a picture. It was the woman he loved and intended to marry.

John took his girlfriend's picture out of his suitcase and placed it on his dresser. "Hey, Tommy, look at this babe. Isn't she a beauty? May is the girl I intend to marry. She is a grade school teacher in Springfield. However, I don't want to be tied down while I'm in college. I want to sow a little wild oats while I'm a junior and senior."

Tommy hesitated a moment then he said, "I intend to go out a few times, but I hope I don't let myself sow oats that are too wild."

The next morning Tommy went to breakfast, then he walked to the Catholic church on the other side of town. He had not been going to church as regularly as when he drove his mother, the twins, and Kay to the Catholic church in Gilmore. This particular morning he felt he needed a little help from God after his Saturday night trip with John.

On Monday morning Tommy attended his organic chemistry class. He had taken general chemistry, qualitative and quantitative chemistry, now he was taking organic chemistry under Dr. Ravely. He enjoyed all his classes at Illinois College, but he wondered how he would do in this particular branch of chemistry, with its complicated formulas and the need for a lot of memorization.

As the weeks went by, Tommy became more and more fascinated by these carbon compounds and their derivatives. It seemed the more complicated the formulas were, the more they intrigued him.

Twelve

The first week went by quickly. Tommy couldn't wait to see Ann and talk to her about her first week of teaching first graders.

Ann said, "Just think, Tommy, here are little boys and girls who are away from their moms and dads for, in many cases, the first time for a whole day. The teacher has the challenge to make it possible for them to concentrate on learning letters and words and numbers, while getting used to spending the day away from home.

"You know, Tommy, I could notice the change every day for the first week. I feel confident that, as the weeks go by, these boys and girls will be eager to go to school, eager to spend time with their new friends and eager to learn."

Tommy said, "Ann, I think you are a born teacher, and the ones who will benefit the most are the children in your class."

"Tommy, thanks for the compliment. Now tell me, where are we going tonight?"

Tommy said, "Lady's choice. You select a place, teach."

Ann said, "Let's go to the show in Gilmore. I saw where Rudolph Valentino is playing in *The Sheik*. Remember, Tommy Victori, Valentino is the great Italian lover."

Tommy said, "That will be alright with me. I'll watch his technique and I'll try it on you know who?"

Ann laughed and said, "Maybe we better go to Hamburg's."

Tommy said, "That will be fine, but we'll go to Hamburg's after the show. By the way, I have a story to tell you, Ann."

Tommy hesitated a minute then he told Ann about his new roommate, John Vana, from Springfield; their trip to the opening school dance; John's girlfriend, May; his introduction to Jane Miller; and his dancing twice with Jane. He also told Ann about their trip to the night spot near Jacksonville, their two glasses of wine, and the trip to the dorm. He added that they were all juniors in school but there was no mugging.

After Tommy's confession, Ann just sat there for a couple of minutes. Then she said, "Tommy, I went to a couple of dances with girlfriends in college. I never told you because there was nothing serious.

"Tommy, if you report back to me after every dance at Illinois College. I know you are my man. I really believe you love me, as I love you."

Tommy said, "Thanks, Ann. You are right."

The Sheik was all it was advertised to be. "Wow," said Tommy, "I can see why they call him 'the great lover.' "

Ann said, "The women say he has 'bedroom eyes.' "

Tommy said, "Let's go to Hamburg's. We can let off a lot of steam."

Ann said, "I wouldn't want to park at the Gilmore Lake after that picture."

Tommy said, "I can stand anything but temptation."

Thirteen

Tommy's junior year went rapidly. Before he knew it was Thanksgiving and then Christmas. Ann would soon be finishing her first semester of teaching. The twins were high school seniors, and Kay was graduating from grade school. Life was moving too rapidly for Mary, who was now in her forties.

Mary had been approached by several single miners and a couple of divorced miners for a supper date at Gilmore, but she had smiled and said, "No." Then one evening after the holidays, when Tommy came home for a weekend, because she wanted Tommy to be present, when she brought up the subject, Mary said, "It will soon be seven years since your dad passed on."

"Tommy, how old are you now?"

Tommy said, "I'll soon be twenty-one."

Mary added, "That makes the twins graduating from high school at eighteen and Kay finishing grade school at fourteen." They all stopped what they were doing and looked at their mother askance.

Tommy was the first one to turn to his mother and ask, "Why are you talking about our ages this evening? There must be a reason."

Mary said, "I notice all of you have friends. Tommy has Ann; the twins had girlfriends; and Kay is starting to have a boyfriend over. Where does that leave me?"

Kay said, "Mom, you have all of us. We all love you dearly."

Mary said, "You are right, but in a few years, you'll be getting married and leaving Hinders. Even if you aren't married, you'll be leaving to get a job. Then too, the mine will close in a few years as all coal mines do, and I'll have to leave, too."

Tommy said, "You can come and live with us."

Mary said, "Thanks, but you have your own lives to lead, and I wouldn't want to be living with any of you."

Tommy asked, "Why are you bringing this up at this time? I'm sure you have a reason."

Mary said, "I wanted all of you to be together before I brought up the subject. You all know how much I loved your dad."

All the children nodded.

Mary continued, "For several years now single men have asked me to go to supper, dances, or a show and I've always said no. What would you do, say, or how would you feel if I started going out?"

They all sat there stunned. Jimmy and an echo, Paul said, "Gee, Mom, I never gave it a thought."

Tommy said, "Mom, your personal life is up to you."

Kay started to cry. Her mother went over and put her arms around Kay. "Don't cry. It won't happen unless all of you okay it."

Mary said, "At the moment there is a single miner who is a motorman like your father was, about my age, who asked me out. What would you say if I asked him to come over some evening for supper so you could meet him and get acquainted?"

Tommy said, "Mother, would you mind leaving the room for a few minutes so we could talk it over?"

Mary got up from her chair in the living room and, without a word, walked into the kitchen. The twins and Kay looked at big brother Tommy for advice. Tommy said, "We have all been taking Mom for granted. Since Dad died, she has been giving all her time to us, even going to jail, trying to make a living for us. Fortunately, the mine started again and she was able to start our store again, pay off the bills and with our help made us a decent standard of living. However, Mom is only in her mid-forties and will have a lot of years ahead of her. As she said she doesn't want to be a burden to us. That is the way things are. What do the rest of you think?"

Paul spoke up, "Tommy, you laid out the facts. Even with us around, we have heard her say many times how lonely she is, and how her tears have wet her pillow through the years."

Jimmy said, "I'm sorry we didn't realize that we have been a little selfish, but there is only one sister and we all want to hear from her."

Kay wiped her eyes and said, "We all want Mother to be happy, so the least we can do is let her invite this man over for supper."

Fourteen

Mary did not want to interfere with the children's week-end plans, but she knew Tommy had to be there. She arranged with Tommy, the twins, and Kay to invite Mike O'Neil over in four weeks, on Sunday. However, she made that tentative because she would have to check with Mike O'Neil. So on a Sunday in February, they were all nervous and on needles and pins from early church to one o'clock, the time Mary's guest was to arrive. Mike drove up in a Model T Ford that looked like the twin of their Model T 1926, the Victori family car.

There was a knock on the door, Mary went over with a big nervous smile on her face as she opened it for Mike O'Neil. An Irishman, nearly six-feet tall, greeted them with a big smile. He had light brown hair and light brown eyes and was so friendly and personable that he made a good impression on all of the children. Tommy stepped forward with a friendly handshake, followed by the twins and a shy Kay who also held out her hand. Mike was a little shorter than Tommy, about the same height as the twins, and, of course, a lot taller than Mary and Kay who were about five-feet-three-inches tall.

Mary brought the food over to the large kitchen table and said, "We will all eat family style. I have coffee and tea to drink. The kids will have tea, and I'll have coffee. What will you have, Mike?"

Mike said, "Coffee, thanks, Mary."

Tommy passed the spaghetti and meatballs, Italian salad, green beans, and corn. Tommy said, "I hope an Irishman like Mr. O'Neil likes Italian food."

Mike said, "I sure do."

Jimmy laughed and said, "Mom always makes plenty, and she'll have no trouble feeding an extra."

"That's right," added Paul.

"My mother is a really good cook," said Kay.

Mary smiled and said, "Let's wait until Mike has eaten, and see what he says."

After they finished their dinner, Mary said, "Let's adjourn to the living room and have our pumpkin pie and a glass of red wine. Kay, we'll even let you have a small glass."

As they were relaxing and drinking their wine, Tommy asked, "Where are you from, Mike?"

Mike said with only a slight Irish brogue, "I was born in Ireland and came to the United States when I was ten years old."

Paul asked, "Have you always worked in coal mines?"

Mike answered, "We came to Illinois, and I have been working in coal mines since I was sixteen years old."

Jimmy said, "Our dad came from Italy, and he worked in coal mines until he was killed in the Hinders Mine riot."

"Yes, I heard about that. It's a sad story," said Mike.

Tommy said, "I'm sure you and Mother will not object if we all leave and go visit friends?"

Kay said, "What about the dishes?"

Mary said, "Don't worry about the dishes. I'll rinse them off and pile them up."

Mike added, "I'll help."

After the children had left, Mary and Mike sat on the living room couch and talked. Mary said, "What do you think of my children?"

Mike answered, "They are a lively, well-behaved bunch."

"I must admit they were not as loud as usual," Mary said.

Mike said, "You would expect that with a stranger present. Mary, let me compliment you on your food. It was delicious."

Mary blushed and said, "Thank you."

He answered by saying, "I'm going to leave in a few minutes so you can do your dishes. I don't want to stay here too long on my first trip."

Mike got up, shook hands with Mary and said, "Would you consider going to a show in Gilmore next weekend?"

Mary answered with a short, "Yes."

Tommy was the first one to return that evening. He said, "Your jovial Irishman seems to be a nice gentleman."

Mary said, "I'm glad you liked him."

Just then, the twins came in. Jimmy said, "We liked Mike."

"That's right," added Paul.

"Mother, as you know, I have my suitcase packed, and the twins are taking me to Gilmore to catch the Illinois Terminal Railroad to Springfield, and then I'll get a bus to Jacksonville." Tommy picked up his suitcase, gave his mother a hug, and said to the twins, "One of you drive. I'll sit in the backseat."

Kay did not come home for another hour.

When she came in, her mother asked, "Did you have a good time?"

Kay replied, "Yes, I did, Mother, but I was thinking about Mike O'Neil, all the time I was gone."

"Well," said Mary, "what conclusion did you draw?"

Kay replied, "He seems to be a nice enough fellow, but I can't picture him as my stepfather."

Mary gave a nervous laugh and said, "Kay, do not be so hasty. I have only met him in the store a few times and here today. Time will tell if anything develops."

Fifteen

When Tommy returned to Jacksonville, his roommate had not returned from his weekend trip to Springfield. Tommy got all his books together, chemistry, calculus, physics, and history of American education. He had sixteen semester hours of what most people would say was a tough schedule. Tommy smiled to himself and thought, *It depends on your aptitude, ability, and interest.* He always liked science and math, but he wasn't sure of his minor in education.

Tommy was about to go to the cafeteria for supper when John Vana came in. Tommy said, "I was about to go to the cafeteria for supper."

John said, "I'm not very hungry, but I'll go along. I want to tell you about May."

Tommy said, "You are sure welcome. I don't like to eat by myself, and Sunday evening there are few there."

Tommy took a light supper, a ham sandwich, a piece of apple pie and a cup of black coffee. He smiled when he remembered the big meal that they had at one o'clock with Mike O'Neil. He noticed that John only took a piece of apple pie and coffee.

After they ate, Tommy and John returned to their room in the dormitory. Tommy was getting ready to pick up his history of education book when John said, "I have to tell someone so you are the one, Tommy.

"My girlfriend, May, has missed her period, and she thinks she is pregnant."

"Wow," said Tommy. "That could be serious."

John said, "We have talked it over and both agree that we must consider an abortion. Yes, we know it is illegal, but May knows that as soon as she shows the Springfield Board of Education will fire her. That might happen even if we get married. If possible, we would prefer a doctor who would be willing to do an abortion. Tommy, do you know of any doctor in the Gilmore area that would perform an abortion? What about a coal mine doctor?"

Tommy said, "Gosh, John, you and May are in a rough situation. However, don't do anything until you find out for sure.

"Would you consider a midwife? I hear that there are several midwives in our mining area that help pregnant women in very early stages."

It took Tommy a long time to go to sleep and he could hear John tossing in his bed. Yet, there was nothing he could do to help John and May.

The next morning he let John sleep while he went to breakfast and then to his eight o'clock chemistry class. When he got back to the dorm, John was gone and he didn't see John until supper. May had called and said that she had a doctor lined up, just in case. They were going to wait until the weekend.

John went home that weekend to Springfield. He was in a state of shock and anxiety. Tommy stayed in Jacksonville that weekend, but John did not come back Sunday or Monday, finally returning on Tuesday. When he saw Tommy, he forced a smile to his face and said, "Everything has been taken care of."

Tommy said, "Let's hope everything works out for the best, John. I'm here to help in any way I can, even if it is only moral support."

John patted Tommy on the back and said, "Thanks."

Sixteen

Tommy had played a lot of baseball in Hinders and had played tag football and a pick-up sides basketball with two orange crate hoops nailed to homemade bankboards for goals, but had not played any sports in high school because he had to hurry home after school to help his mother in the store.

However, when he got to college, he became a fan of the Blueboys, taking in a fair number of games. Illinois College belonged to the little nineteen, meaning nineteen little colleges.

He invited John to go to a basketball game with him at the Illinois School for the Deaf's gymnasium. The Illinois College gym was to small for the college games. It was Friday night and they had both decided to spend the weekend in Jacksonville and study. Illinois College was playing Milliken from Decatur. Milliken was favored to win, but since it was a home game, Illinois College had some hope. Illinois College got off to a good start and was leading at the end of the first half. Then, Milliken caught up by the middle of the second half. From then to the end of the game, the lead changed hands several times.

Tommy and John were in the cheering section, clapping and participating with the cheerleaders in the yells. There were only thirty seconds left when Illinois College got the rebound and the score was tied. Fletcher, the best scoring Illinois College guard, had the ball. Everyone knew Illinois College was going to hold the ball for one last shot. There were only ten seconds left when Fletcher started driving for the basket. Two Milliken men came after him. At the last second, he passed to "Too Tall Jones," the Illinois College center, who dunked it.

The crowd was on their feet as the home team rushed to congratulate each other. John was relaxing and enjoying himself for the first time in a couple of weeks. He grabbed Tommy and said, "Let's go have a cold one."

It was spring and the twins, Paul and Jimmy, were looking forward to graduation. Tommy was home for the weekend and the twins cornered him.

"What's up?" asked Tommy.

Jimmy spoke first, "We know that you plan to go out with Ann, and we don't blame you, but are hoping that you would go out with us one Saturday night before we graduate from high school."

Paul said, "Surely, that is not asking too much."

Tommy smiled and said, "That can be arranged. I'll tell Ann, and we'll plan for one Saturday night in April."

"Remember," said Jimmy, "we mean just the three of us."

"The three of us it shall be," answered Tommy.

Seventeen

Each weekend when Tommy came home, the twins confronted him. Tommy finally arranged with Ann to give the last Saturday in April to the twins.

When the last Saturday in April came, Tommy ate supper at home with his mother, the twins, and Kay. Mary and Kay knew that this was the twins' night with Tommy. They all laughed about it and Tommy told the twins, out of earshot of his mother and Kay, "I'm willing to have fun, but I won't do anything that would make Mother ashamed of us."

Jimmy laughed and said, "We did not plan on going to Maggie's or any red light district in any other town."

Paul said, "All we planned was a show and going to a couple of taverns for a beer."

"That's right," said Jimmy.

Tommy asked, "How do you know they'll serve you?"

Paul added, "We know that the prohibition is still here and all taverns are illegal, but we have been around here and we know what taverns still serve seniors in high school."

Jimmy and Paul got in the front seat of the car. Jimmy was at the wheel.

"Where are we going?" asked Tommy.

"We're going to Carmount to see Charlie Chaplin in *The Goldrush*," answered Paul.

"That is okay with me," said Tommy. "However, I'll drive when we leave the first tavern. I only intend to drink Coke. I want to get home in one piece, and don't try to change that because I already promised Mom I wouldn't drink. Don't think you'll put anything over on her. She could smell the home brew when you guys came home after a couple of drinks."

Jimmy grabbed the wheel and said, "Wow, I didn't know Mom knew."

"Neither did I," said Paul. "How come she didn't say anything?"

Tommy said, "Mom is smarter than you give her credit for. She trusted you guys to use good judgment. If you had come home drunk, she would have scolded you."

"Let's change the subject," said Jimmy. "You know that we both decided to go to Carmount College. Ann recommends it highly, and it will be a lot cheaper for us."

"I think that is a good move," said Tommy.

In a few minutes, they pulled up near the Lyric Theater in Carmount. Tommy got out and bought three adult tickets and they went in and sat on the right side, about half way down.

They got a lot of laughs out of Charlie Chaplin. He looked undersized and undernourished. Chaplin wore a battered derby hat, a coat too small for him, and pants much too large. He walked in a shuffling manner that suggested he never wore a pair of shoes his own size. He became one of the most famous stars in motion picture history.

"He is really comical," said Jimmy.

"The best there is," said Paul.

"This is one time I have to agree with you," said Tommy. "Now where do we go?"

"Just sit back and relax, Tommy. I'm driving," said Jimmy. They got to the outskirts of Carmount and went down a side road where two taverns were located, about one mile from State Road 4.

Jimmy pulled up and said, "Here we are."

They got out and went into a large tavern with a bar, a dozen stools, and a dozen tables. Tommy said, "This place wasn't here when I was in high school."

Tommy saw a couple dozen high school and college students drinking. They sat down on three stools along the bar. They ordered two beers and a Coke. The bartender brought them two foamy mugs and a Coke. They looked around. The twins recognized a few friends. Even Tommy knew a few of the drinkers. There was a man at the piano playing and singing with a strong voice and a good deal of volume.

Jimmy said, "That's Rudy Pines. He is usually here on Saturday night. He brings a crowd."

Two couples who were at a table motioned for them to come over. There were only two empty seats, so one of the men grabbed a chair from another table and made room for a seventh chair at the table.

Tommy and the twins went over and sat down. Jimmy and Paul introduced Tommy, "This is our big brother who is in college. We are introducing him to some of the night spots around Carmount."

Tommy said, "Hi." Then he sat back and sipped his Coke. He felt out of it since they all seemed to be of high school age.

They sat there for half an hour over the one beer for which they paid ten cents. Then they told the waitress that they all wanted a second beer, except Tommy who ordered another Coke. They all looked at Tommy askance, but Tommy said nothing.

After the Victoris finished their drinks, they left and walked down the road to the second tavern. It was about the same size as the first tavern. This time they sat at the bar and did not move after ordering two beers and a

Coke. Within half an hour, they got in their Model T Ford and headed for home.

Jimmy said, "Thanks for coming along, Tommy, and driving home, but I'm afraid that your promise to Mom made for a dull evening."

Tommy replied, "Not at all." He kept driving.

When they got home after midnight, Mary was waiting up for them and welcomed them home. Tommy was glad that he kept his promise to his mother.

Eighteen

Mary had gone to the theater and out to supper several times with Mike O'Neil. Mike always drove up in front of the store, walked to the back door, knocked, and was welcomed in by Mary. Mary and Mike were getting better and better acquainted. Mary had asked Mike if he had ever been married.

Mike said, "No, but I came close a couple of times. Yes, I'm forty-five years old and should be married and have a family. I came from a large Irish family. I have two brothers and two sisters, and I'm the only one who never married. In fact, I think my family has given up on me. They think I'll be a bachelor all my life."

Mary said, "When I came to the coal mining area of Illinois, there were several thousand miners from many of the countries of Europe and only a small number of eligible women. In fact, many of the miners went back to their home country, married, and brought wives with them to the United States.

"As it turned out, my husband, Marion, and I met on the boat coming from Italy. Marion had decided to see what there was for him in New York. We parted at the boat. Marion considered New York too big and too unfriendly. I had given him my sister's address where I was going in Illinois. He came to Kollinson, Illinois, got a job in the coal mine, and looked me up.

"Fortunately, we both spoke Italian and had no trouble renewing our acquaintance. The upshot was we got married and started a family in Kollinson. Marion was a motorman just like you. However, Marion had developed a cough from the coal dust, and we decided to try Hinders. Marion got a job at the Hinders Mine. We built a building with a store front and living quarters in back in order to have a country store so Marion could quit the mine." By now Mary was getting emotional.

Mike came over, put his arms around Mary and said, "If you are ready, Mary, we will go to the new Greek restaurant in Gilmore. I understand that they really serve tasty food."

He helped Mary with her coat. Then they walked to Mike's Model T and headed for Gilmore.

Kay was trying to accept Mike O'Neil as her mother's friend. In her mind, the word "friend" was almost acceptable. The word "boyfriend" was not. Nothing that indicated that the word "friend" might become "suitor," a man courting or wooing a woman, was permissible in her mind. Kay could not visualize her mother being kissed by or kissing another man. Although, she was only six when her father died, she still remembered how Marion would pick her up, kiss her, and call her his doll. Kay was the only girl in a family with three boys. She was the youngest and received the most attention. She knew her thoughts were not fair to her mother and fought with the idea that her mother must not be too intimate with another man. However, the more her mother saw of Mike, the less she liked it.

Mike did his best to win Kay over. He was friendly without being too friendly. At times, they invited Kay to go along shopping. He tried to buy her a little something without much success. Mike knew that he had to continue trying, however.

The boys seemed to be accepting him much better. However, he did not neglect them. Mike always included them in the conversation when they were around. He laughed and talked with them. Mary also tried to help, but she realized they were not making too much progress with Kay.

Nineteen

Tommy's junior year in college was rapidly drawing to a close. His relationship with his roommate, John, had grown closer since John confided in him about his girl-friend's pregnancy.

John said to Tommy, "We both have girlfriends who are teachers, and they have never met. Why don't we invite them for the last school dance of the year, a week from Saturday?"

"That sounds like a good idea to me," answered Tommy.

"We can get them a room at the Jacksonville Hotel, and they can stay overnight."

Tommy said, "I'll check with Ann this weekend, and you can make arrangements with May."

On the Saturday of the dance, John and Tommy made two trips to the bus depot in John's Dodge, one to pick up May, and a second trip with the three of them to pick up Ann. After introductions, May got into the front seat with John, and Ann got into the back seat with Tommy.

John said, "We'll take you to your hotel to check in, and we'll wait for you in the lounge. Then we'll take you to the Illinois College campus and supper at Moore's Café where Tommy worked as a waiter for a couple of years."

Tommy said, "We have what we hope will be an enjoyable evening planned for you ladies."

May said, "We are not going to be hard to please."

Ann added, "May's right. As long as we are with you two men, I think we will be happy."

John drove down State Street and then over to College. Ann looked out at the big beautiful homes and said, "Tommy and I come from Hinders, a coal mining town, where the houses are only four and five rooms and all the homes are wooden. The only big home in town was built by Mr. Hinders, who founded the town, and is now owned by the new mine owner, Mr. John Sampson. These homes look so large and stately that I can't image what they look like inside."

Tommy said, "There are sections of Jacksonville where poorer people live and the negro section that the houses are not so big and luxurious."

May added, "Springfield, being the state capital, has it all from the biggest homes to the poor areas where you wouldn't want to live."

John said, "Talking about capitals, I have been to Washington, D.C. You see some of the best houses in the world in Washington and areas that are not fit to live in."

Tommy said, "Here we are at the campus on the hill. We plan to park at our dormitory, show you our room, and then walk around the campus."

Hand in hand, Tommy and Ann, and John and May enjoyed their walk. The spring air was invigorating. The leaves on the trees were green and the color of the grass matched. They stopped in Crampton Hall, Jones Chapel, and Sturtevant and then got back in the car to head uptown to Moore's Café, one block south of the Jacksonville square.

Tommy had called Moore's Café to make reservations, and Mr. Moore himself greeted them. Tommy introduced Ann and May to Mr. Moore. He already had met John. Mr. Moore was an impressive host, always dressed in a tailor made suit, white shirt with gold cuffs and spats that matched the color of his shoes. He told Ann

47

that he was proud of Tommy and he called him one of his boys.

After a pleasant dinner, they went back to the hotel to freshen up and wait for the college dance. At the dance, Tommy and Ann and John and May danced the first couple of dances together, then they traded partners. They decided to sit the next dance out and talk.

Ann asked, "Tommy aren't you going to introduce me to Jane Miller or is she here?"

Tommy said, "If you have no objection, I'll ask her for a dance, and then I'll bring her over."

John said, "I'll do the same with Sarah."

A couple of dances later, Ann and May got their wish. They met Jane and Sarah. After the introductions, Tommy and John got up and gave their seats to Jane and Sarah. Tommy and John went out for a little fresh air. When they came back in the women were carrying on a lively conversation. When Tommy and John approached the ladies, Jane and Sarah got up and gave Tommy and John back their seats. After a few pleasant words and smiles, the women went back with their friends.

Ann was the first to speak, "Tommy, you never told me what a beauty Jane was."

Before the men could reply May chimed in with, "John, I think Sarah is every bit as pretty as Jane."

Tommy said, "They are not bad for second choice."

John added, "Tommy is right; when we can't have the best, we get the second best."

Then they all laughed and the girls said, "Let's dance."

After the dance, May said, "Are you going to take us to the night spot outside the Jacksonville city limits where you took Sarah and Jane? Ann, do you want to go there?"

48

Ann replied, "Gosh, May, I'd like to go there but do you think two school teachers should break the Volsted Act that makes liquor illegal?"

John said, "The Volsted Act prohibits the manufacture, sale or transportation of intoxicating liquors within the United States."

Tommy said, "John and I have already talked it over and if you ladies have no objection we'll take you to the night spot and we'll all order Cokes; at least you'll see how the other half lives."

John pulled over on the side of the road, stopped and asked, "What do you ladies want to do? We have some nice restaurants where we could have Cokes and a bite to eat."

May spoke up and said, "Why don't we do both? Go out to the night spot, have a Coke, and then have a little to eat."

"That sounds good to me," said Ann.

John drove back on the highway and headed for Sammy's, the night club. It was already crowded with people from the dance, but Tommy and John managed to find an empty table. They all sat down and Tommy ordered four Cokes.

The girls looked around and saw a bar and at least twenty tables. They looked to see what people near them were drinking and quickly concluded that wine and beer were the preferred beverages.

John and Tommy were trying to relax and set a good example for the ladies. Ann and May sipped their sodas and seemed to be enjoying themselves. After a couple Cokes, they departed for Jacksonville to Jerry's Restaurant for a night snack.

"We can't come up to your rooms unless we are registered as husband and wife," said John.

Ann said, "We'll wait until our honeymoon for that."

May chipped in, "I agree."

The next morning after a late breakfast, John and Tommy took the girls to the bus station and waited with them until their buses arrived.

Twenty

Mary said to Tommy, the twins, and Kay, "We sure have plenty on the next two weekends. Kay graduates from grade school, and the twins graduate from high school. And next year, Tommy graduates from college."

Tommy said, "You are right about the next two weekends being busy, but Mom, it'll be a whole year before I get my diploma from Illinois College. So please don't run the next two weeks in with the next year."

Mary laughed and then asked, "Is it alright if I invite Mike O'Neil to the two graduations and the two parties?"

The twins almost shouted, "Mom, you are still the boss of this family. Invite anybody you want. Don't you agree, Kay?"

Kay put in, "You twins are two-thirds of the graduates, so I'll make it unanimous. However, when it comes to planning the parties, I'm sure Mother will do the work with a little help from me."

Tommy, who was listening, said, "Go ahead, Mother. You are in charge. I'll invite Ann and the twins can make their choices, oh, and that applies to Kay, too."

One would think that Mary was preparing for New Year's Eve if they had seen her buying balloons and noise makers of various kinds. Indeed, she was happier than she had been in six years. The children were getting along with their education; the store was bringing in more money; and Mike O'Neil was providing companionship. Although she realized that Mike was expecting more than just companionship, she had not made up her mind.

She decided that she should keep her mind busy with the two parties, including the food and drinks to be purchased. Mike was coming over the two Wednesday nights before the two Fridays of graduation. That did not pose much of a problem since they were going out both Wednesdays. What did concern her was that Mike had been insisting on more intimate hugs and kisses and had told her last week that an Irishman would want more, and she also realized that she too wanted more.

The graduation at Hinders two-room elementary school was short. Miss Green played the piano for a couple of songs. The valedictorian gave a short speech and Miss Kaiser handed out ten diplomas. Mary Victori thought, *My kids were lucky having Miss Green and Miss Kaiser all these years. Usually country school teachers do not stay in one school very long.*

The Victoris and their guests hurried over to the Victoris' store. Mary had balloons of various colors and red, white, and blue crepe paper in the shape of a tent in the large store front. There were plenty of tables, sandwiches, salami, and numerous cheeses, and soda for the children to drink and wine for the adults.

Mary still had her player piano from when she and Marion and friends had private dances, and she and Mike O'Neil led the dancing. Tommy and Ann, Jimmy and Paul and their girlfriends, and even Kay had a freshman boy over and danced. The dancing and fun went on till ten o'clock.

The following Friday, they went to the Gilmore High School in two Model T Fords, one belonging to the Victori family and the other to Mike O'Neil. Mary and Mike went in Mike's car with Kay and her freshman boyfriend sitting in the back seat. Tommy and Ann were in the front and the twins and their girlfriends in the back of the Victori car.

The high school graduation lasted nearly two hours with the valedictorian and the salutatorian giving talks, a processional, singing, the commencement speaker, the handling out of one hundred diplomas, and a recessional. There was a lot of clapping, and it sounded particularly loud when the Victori group chimed in when the only twins in the class graduated.

At last it was over. To the surprise of everyone, Mary had rented Hamburg's Hall for Friday night, and the party was sponsored by the miners union in honor of Marion Victori's twin sons who were graduating from high school.

Jones, who was president of the union, made a talk about how Marion Victori's death had brought the town and the union together. Then Jones had Mary Victori come forward with her two sons and handed them each a one-hundred-dollar scholarship. Mary was in tears. It took a full minute before she could take control of herself, and then she and Jimmy and Paul thanked Mr. Jones and the union.

The graduation party went on until midnight. Finally, Mike O'Neil took an exhausted Mary home. She went to sleep and never even heard the children come home later.

Twenty-one

As Tommy entered the cage and grabbed the hook with his left hand to steady him while the cage descended, he thought, *This is my fourth summer working as assistant to the surveyor, John Combs. Next summer will be my fifth and last.* If everything worked as planned, he hoped to be teaching chemistry and physics the fall after graduation. He planned to enter Lincoln Law School in the fall of 1928, riding the Illinois Terminal to Springfield at night. He planned to marry Ann in 1929 and buy one of those Model A Fords, then he could drive to Springfield part of the time. He hoped that the plan he and Jack Wenz, an elementary teacher at Gilmore, came up with would work, as they would attend Lincoln Law School together.

John Combs was talking to him. Tommy blushed as he asked John to repeat what he had said. John laughed and said, "Daydreaming?"

Tommy replied, "I'm afraid you are right. I'm sorry."

John said, "On this job, you better keep your mind on your work at all times, or you could get hurt."

Tommy said, "You are right. I should bend over and let you give me a boot."

John replied, "The next time, I will."

As they got off, John said, "We are nearing the spot where they dug into the old Tom Mine a few years ago and lost five men. I've been checking old Tom's surveys, and I'm not sure they are correct. Therefore, we will check and recheck leaving plenty of room for error. So,

Tommy, we must be more careful than ever because we'll be responsible for our own lives and the lives of a number of miners."

Tommy said, "Thank you for the information. You can bet the family jewels that I'll be very careful."

When they took their survey to the office after the whistle blew quitting time, Tommy spent an extra hour with John who thanked Tommy for being so diligent.

Tommy got home so late that the family had already eaten, and Mary was keeping supper warm for him. Tommy explained his tardiness to his mother, who was really impressed with her son.

Tommy could tell that his mother had something on her mind. So he said, "What's up, Mom?"

Mary asked, "Does it show that much?"

"It sure does," Tommy answered.

"Well, Tommy, I knew it was coming. Mike O'Neil wants to marry me."

Tommy answered, "We knew it was coming, too."

Mary said, "If you all knew it was coming, I'll accept his engagement ring and plan a spring wedding. I'll tell the rest of the family this evening before bedtime."

After Tommy ate and Mary did the dishes, she called up Mike O'Neil and said that she would like to see him.

Mike was at the Victoris' at eight o'clock. She met him with a hug and kiss. Mary said, "I told Tommy about our coming engagement. He said the whole family was expecting it. So we will go ahead with the announcement if it's alright with you."

Mike took Mary in his arms and said, "I'm the one who asked in the first place. I'm absolutely thrilled to realize that I'm not only marrying you, but I'm getting a wonderful family besides."

Mary brought in two glasses and a bottle of wine. Then she poured wine in the two glasses and she said, "Let us drink to our engagement." Their glasses touched and they both lifted them as they drank happily.

Mike said, "I felt that you would say yes. I have a surprise for you." He went to his coat and took out a box, opened it up, and Mary saw a beautiful engagement ring. She stood there in a trance as Mike slipped the engagement ring on her finger. With joy in their hearts, they drank another glass of wine, poured by Mike this time.

Twenty-two

Mary caught the twins together and told them about her engagement ring. Paul was the first to hug and kiss his mother and he said, "Good luck, Mom."

Jimmy followed with a hug and kiss and said, "I hope you'll be happy, Mom."

Mary had cautioned her sons not to tell Kay, as she wanted to tell her daughter herself.

That evening when Kay came home, Mary took off her ring and went over and sat next to Kay. "Kay, I have something to tell you."

Kay looked at her mother apprehensively. Mary waited until she had Kay's full attention, and then said, "Mike O'Neil was here this evening. He asked me to marry him, and when I accepted, he gave me an engagement ring."

Kay just sat there stupefied, not knowing what to say.

Mary continued, "This will be a long engagement. We won't get married for over six months, probably sometime after Christmas, maybe next spring."

Kay did her best to hold back the tears and finally said, "Mom, I want you to be happy."

Mary said, "Tommy, Paul, and Jimmy said the same thing."

Paul and Jimmy went out to look for summer jobs on the Monday after graduation. They tried the mines without success. On Tuesday, they tried the shoe factory and the radiator plant in Litchfield but still had no luck.

Mary said, "Why don't you see what you can get at the grocery stores? You can tell them that you have had experience. That might help."

On Wednesday, they went to half a dozen grocery stores in Gilmore. They were offered Saturday jobs at the large cooperative store in Gilmore. They did not reject the job, nor accept it. They told the co-op manager that they would think about it and let him know by Wednesday.

On Saturday morning, they both reported for work at the co-op. The manager said, "I'll take you to the store room and you fellows can work together bringing groceries in push carts, and every Saturday you can restack the shelves. You can do that every Saturday from eight A.M. to five P.M. with an hour off at noon. You'll make three dollars and fifty cents a day."

The twins were not too happy with their jobs but they worked all the first Saturday. Working together, they at least had fun kidding each other about all the money they were making. Jimmy said, "Let's see if I take my girlfriend to the show on Saturday night. It costs twenty-five cents each, a nickel for a bag of popcorn, ten cents for a large hamburger and five cents for a Coke at Jasper's. Multiply all that by two and Saturday night will cost me ninety cents. As Mom would say, the wages are better than nothing."

Paul said, "We have Monday through Friday to look for another job. Who knows, we might get lucky."

Meanwhile, Mary and Kay worked every day in the store, and Tommy continued with his job as assistant surveyor.

Twenty-three

The summer passed by quickly. In August everyone had to buy clothing, the twins to start college, Kay for high school and Tommy for his senior year in college.

Tommy told his mother, "I was hoping I could have a car for my last year in college. Did you see that new Model A that Ford has?"

Mary said, "The new 1928s are out, but they cost over five hundred dollars. I was hoping we could trade in our Model T and get a new 1928 Model A."

Tommy said, "That would be wonderful, Mother, we could use it as a family car."

"Tommy, I wish we could get you an old Dodge like your roommate has for your last year in college. It should cost less than two hundred. Why don't you go to the Dodge garage and check?"

Tommy said, "Mother, that is just wishful thinking. With the twins in college and Kay in high school, we'll be lucky to have the new Model A for a family car."

"Tommy, we have lived frugally and I have saved a little money, so I want you to go to the Dodge garage and see what they want for a Dodge that is three or four years old. When you are home, you'll have to share it with the twins."

The twins started Carmount College. Tommy was driving with his mother in front and Kay and the twins were in the back. In twenty minutes, they were in Carmount and after a few minutes of city driving they pulled up at the Registrar's. The twins went in while Mary,

59

Tommy, and Kay waited outside. They then went over to Hud's Hall, the boys' dorm.

Kay said, "We want to see your room. We saw Tommy's when he started Illinois College."

Mary said, "We all want to see the room."

Tommy said, "You guys are lucky. You are twins. You won't be lonesome. I was one lonely guy the first few weeks in college."

The room was a typical college room: two single beds, two dressers, two chests of drawers, and two desks with reading lamps. After they brought up the boxes and suitcases and Mary helped the twins put their clothes away, she, Tommy, and Kay departed.

Kay said, "I don't know why this is not as sad as when we left Tommy in Jacksonville. Tommy, do you know we all cried when we got home?"

Tommy said, "I shed some tears, too."

Their mother said, "Tommy was the oldest and the first one to leave the nest, and Jacksonville was strange and ten times as far away."

"I guess you are right," chimed in Kay.

When they got home, Mary said, "I'm glad Carmount College started a week early. I haven't had time to look at the new 1928 Model A Fords and Tommy, with Illinois College starting in a week, you haven't gone to the Dodge garage."

Tommy replied, "We'll get your car first. I'm in no hurry. I called John Vana. He and I are going to be roommates again this year, and he says his old Dodge still runs."

Tommy was glad to see John Vana again. "What did you do this summer, John? I worked as an assistant surveyor for the Superior Mine, my fourth summer."

John answered, "Tommy, I worked for the State of Illinois in the Secretary of State's Office in the license department, my second summer."

"Have you registered yet, John?"

"As you know, we pre-registered last spring in my program of social studies. I made no changes."

Tommy said, "In my science field, I made no changes, but I wasn't able to register in educational psychology, which is required. I had a conflict. So I went over to see Dr. Wright and he was very accommodating. He said if there was no other way, he would take care of me in a peripatetic walking class. We could go for a walk twice a week if the weather is good and stay in the office when weather is bad. I'll probably be the only one in class. That was sure nice of him."

"It was more than nice," answered John. "It was a big sacrifice on his part."

"You going to the school dance on Saturday night?" asked Tommy.

"Sure," said John.

"Are you staying here this weekend, Tommy?"

"I sure am," said Tommy.

That weekend, Tommy and John were busy on the dance floor. Both of them danced nearly every dance. They danced several times with Jane Miller and Sarah Sands.

Tommy said to John, "I hope we are going out for a cold one without the girls."

John answered, "We'll go out alone. There is a new night club outside of town that we'll take in."

They rode out of Jacksonville a couple of miles in John's Dodge. John had been given directions how to find this new place. They came to a two-story house with a few cars parked around it and got out.

Tommy said, "I don't like the looks of this place."

John replied, "Tommy, we are two white males, twenty-one years old. What do we have to be afraid of?"

They entered and looked around. There was a bar with ten stools and ten tables with red tablecloths. There were four men on stools, and about half the tables were occupied by men and half a dozen women were seated with the men. Tommy and John ordered a beer at the bar.

They were about half done with their beers when two of the women came from the tables and sat down, one on each side of them. They realized immediately that the gals were women of the night. They decided to tough it out.

The woman near Tommy said, "Can I have a beer?"

The woman near John asked the same question.

"Why not?" asked John.

"Okay by me," said Tommy.

After a couple of sips of beer, each woman put an arm around John and Tommy and said, "We have beds upstairs."

Both men said, "I'm not interested."

The women finished their beers and went back to the tables.

Tommy and John finished their beers, hastily left, and hurried to the Dodge.

Tommy asked, "Did you know this was a house of prostitution?"

John answered, "No, but I wasn't too surprised. It is not a new experience for me. I live in Springfield."

Tommy said, "We have them in Hinders, too. I've never been in one, but we have tried to look in through the windows."

Then Tommy told John about the night the boys from the Hoodlum Club had gone with Harry and Tony. How Harry and Tony went to Maggie's, had been approached by two of the whores, who scared the two young men, by putting an arm around them and taking them to the bar for a drink. Harry and Tony had escaped by running out of Maggie's.

John got a big laugh out of the story.

"I don't know if I'll tell Ann," said Tommy.

"I don't know if I'll tell May," echoed John.

As they were in their beds ready to say goodnight, Tommy said, "I know I'll eventually tell Ann."

"I will tell May, too," echoed John.

Twenty-four

The romance between Mary and Mike O'Neil moved right along. Mary was careful not to spend too much time alone with Mike in private. In public places, she was relaxed; in the theater, at Hamburg's, shopping, and at home when the kids were present. When they came home late, she always made a point not to invite Mike in. Parking was another matter. Mike couldn't keep his hands off of her.

Mike finally said, "Are we going to have sex before we get married?"

Mary answered, "No way. How can I tell my children about sex unless I set a good example?"

A disappointed Mike took Mary home early that night and stayed away for a week. He finally came back with a sheepish smile on his face and said, "I agree to live by your terms."

Mary said, "You are welcome back." She then gave him a hug and kiss. It was Saturday night, and they decided to go to Hamburg's to dance.

Mike said, "Now that Tommy and the twins are in college, you only have Kay at home."

Mary said, "Yes, and the place seems empty." She realized, as soon as the words came out of her mouth, that she had put her foot in it.

Mike said, "I'll come over."

Mary came back with, "After we are married, you can sleep in my room and in my bed."

Mike said, "We can't get married tomorrow. Would it be alright if I take off of work on Monday and we go to Carmount Monday and have the justice of the peace marry us?"

Mary said, "Let's dance."

Twenty-five

The twins were giving their college professors a fit. They registered for the same classes and they dressed alike. The professors couldn't tell them apart. More than once, a professor said Jimmy when it was Paul and vice-versa. They decided to answer when the instructor pointed, regardless of the name used.

They decided to major in mathematics as they had better aptitude for the subject than English and social studies. The first week went by quickly, and in the second week initiation began. Since they had to work fifteen hours a week, they were both assigned to the cafeteria. They did more than their fair share of pots and pans.

The sophomores in the dorm had them shine their shoes, do their laundry, and all week long, during initiation week, they had prayer meetings where the freshmen were sent on errands and wild goose chases such as going to the tobacco store and bringing back a package of cigarettes or going to a saloon and bringing a Coke or going to the girls' dorm and bringing back the signature of a confessed virgin.

The twins were glad when initiation week was over. Friday night they had a big dance. The twins had their training at Hamburg's and they were both good dancers. They had a good night.

On Sunday, Mary and Kay picked them up in the Victoris' 1928 Model A Ford. The twins fell in love with the new Ford and each wanted to drive. Mary took a coin out of her purse and said, "Paul, you call it. The winner gets to drive home. The loser drives back."

Jimmy won with heads.

Paul got into the front seat with his twin. Mary and Kay gladly got into the back.

Kay said, "You have been here two weeks. Tell us all about those two weeks."

Jimmy said, "The school work went fine. We were assigned to the cafeteria for the work program. We are the 'pots and pans boys.' "

Mary and Kay laughed and Mary said, "That should teach you to be a lot of help at home."

Jimmy said, "Please, Mom."

Paul said, "Last week was initiation week. The sophomores in the dormitory really took advantage of us. They ran us on all kinds of errands from running uptown for cigarettes to going to the girls' dorm for a pair of undies. It was all in fun, and looking back, it wasn't too bad."

Kay asked, "What are you going to do this weekend?"

Jimmy said, "We are going to drop in on our girlfriends, Mabel and Nancy, and probably end up at Hamburg's."

Kay looked forward to high school as a real promotion. She was leaving the kid's stage and becoming an adult. She felt more grown up. It was a good feeling to a fourteen-year-old girl.

She registered for English, algebra, general science, Spanish, and physical education. The first week she became acquainted with five new teachers. That was a big change for a student who had only two teachers in her first eight years of school.

Six of the graduates of Hinders were going to Gilmore High School. That meant that Kay had to get acquainted with over a hundred freshmen in her class. She was a good student and a good mixer so she looked forward to the school year.

Kay also knew a sophomore boy from Hinders by the name of Harry Barnes, who she had over at her graduation party. Since they had no classes together, they had agreed to meet in the cafeteria at lunch. Kay hurried over to the cafeteria when the bell rang dismissing the students at noon. As agreed, Harry was waiting for her and they got in the lunch line together. Kay had told her mother not to prepare a sack lunch the first day, as she was going to try the cafeteria.

Harry said, "Kay, how did you like your first morning in high school?"

Kay said, "It was fun, but I have a lot to learn."

Harry laughed and said, "Don't worry. It takes time, but you won't have much trouble."

After lunch, Kay went to her afternoon classes. She had never been in a physical education class. After listening to the teacher tell about the exercise, games, and activities they would participate in, she told herself that the class would be fun.

It took Kay about a week to get into the high school routine and she told her mother, "I'm going to like high school."

Twenty-six

Tommy and John continued going to college dances, which they seemed to enjoy by playing the field, dancing with numerous young ladies. Then one evening there was a call from the MacMurray College for Women, on the east side of Jacksonville, from women who wanted them to attend a dance.

Tommy said, "I have never gone to a MacMurray College dance."

John said, "I have. You can have a lot of fun. You should go, Tommy, at least one time in your four years at Illinois College."

Tommy said, "I don't know if I should."

John urged, "Let me call our names in. All Illinois College students are eligible. I'll show you the ropes."

Tommy said, "I'll try it one time."

Tommy found himself riding in John's Dodge over to MacMurray College that Friday night. They showed their Illinois College identification cards at the door and were admitted. They walked over the men's side and sat down.

John said, "Since we don't know any women, we'll just sit here and wait."

When the first dance started, the women came over to ask for a dance. Most of the ladies already knew most of the men from Illinois College, including John. There was a surplus of women. A blonde came up to Tommy and said, "Dance?"

Tommy stood up and said, "My name is Tommy Victori."

The young lady said, "I'm Doris Kent from Hillsboro, Illinois."

She danced well, and she and Tommy got along well together. She asked Tommy for the next dance and Tommy said, "That's fine with me. By the way, I'm from Hinders, a coal mine town near Gilmore, Illinois."

Doris said, "I'm glad you mentioned Gilmore because I never heard of Hinders."

Tommy replied, "That does not surprise me. The town is rather small."

When the dance was over, Tommy thanked her and said, "You are a good dancer. I'd like to have another dance later."

Doris replied, "You do very well. It would be a pleasure."

Tommy and John danced until eleven o'clock, when the dance ended.

Tommy danced the last dance with Doris. She said, "Will I see you here again?"

Tommy answered, "I enjoyed myself, but I don't usually go to many school dances, as I go home often on weekends."

"A steady girlfriend?" asked Doris.

"That's right," answered Tommy. "Thanks a lot."

Tommy suggested, "Let's stop by at Moore's Café. They stay open until midnight. I'm buying."

John replied, "That suits me."

Tommy looked around. He knew that Mr. Moore lived by the old ditty "early to bed and early to rise, makes a man healthy, wealthy, and wise." Tommy said, "And it has worked for him."

They each ordered a ham sandwich and a Coke. After they finished their sandwich and drinks, they headed back to the college.

The next morning after breakfast, Tommy said to John, "You have told me several times how old this car is."

John said, "Since the Dodge '28 is out, I'll tell you again. This Dodge is a '23. It's five years old and runs like a clock, as you should know."

Tommy asked, "What would I have to pay for a '23 or '24 in good shape?"

John said, "Two hundred dollars or less."

Tommy answered, "Take me to the bus station. I'm going to surprise Mom. She's been after me to buy a Dodge like yours. Any suggestions?"

"Yes," said John. "Listen to the motor, check the brakes and tires, check the body, and make sure the radiator doesn't leak."

Tommy said, "Why don't you take me home and help me pick out a good Dodge? We'll stop in Carmount and Gilmore."

John said, "Okay."

They packed their suitcases and departed.

When Tommy and John reached Carmount and found the Dodge garage, they talked to a salesman and told him what kind of Dodge they were looking for. They found a 1924 Dodge that met all the tests John outlined.

Tommy said, "How much are you asking?"

The salesman said, "Three hundred dollars, and it's yours."

Tommy said, "I'm from Hinders and got to check there first, but this looks good."

"Remember," said the salesman, "we can't hold it for you."

They got back in John's Dodge and headed for Gilmore, a distance of six miles.

They went back on State Route 4 and headed for Gilmore and went straight to the Dodge garage. They found used 1923 and '24 Dodges that checked out.

Tommy said, "You say that I can have this 1924 Dodge for three hundred dollars?"

"That's right," said the salesman.

Tommy said, "My name is Tommy Victori, and I just live three miles from here. Is it alright if I drive the Dodge home and show it to my mother?"

The salesman said, "I'm familiar with the Victori name, and I've seen you around, Tommy. Sure, drive it home and get your mother's opinion."

Tommy and John got in the 1924 Dodge and Tommy didn't stop until he pulled up in front of the Victori store.

Tommy went in and brought his mother and Kay out. They looked at the car inside and out.

Mary said, "How much do they want?"

Tommy said, "Three hundred dollars."

Mary said, "Offer them two hundred and fifty dollars for it."

"Okay, Mother," said Tommy.

Mary said, "Come inside," to Tommy and John. Mary came back with two hundred and fifty dollars in cash.

Tommy said, "Thanks, Mom. I'll see what the salesman says."

They drove back to the Dodge garage. After a little discussion, the salesman said, "Two hundred and seventy-five dollars, minimum."

Tommy said, "Write up the sales slip. I'll give you two hundred fifty dollars now, and I'll bring you the twenty-five next weekend when I come back from Jacksonville."

"That will be alright," said the salesman.

When they got back to the Victoris' John said to Mrs. Victori, "I'll head to Springfield if you will excuse me?"

Mrs. Victori said, "Come in for a sandwich and a Coke then you can head to Springfield."

They all went in and ate and drank. Then John said, "Thank you very much."

Mary said, "We should thank you. You drove many miles out of your way to bring Tommy home."

Tommy walked John to his car and said, "Thanks, John." He shook his friend's hand and gave him a hug.

The twins came home from Carmount for the weekend, after working at the college on Saturday, with a friend who was coming to Hinders.

There was still enough daylight for the twins to get a good look at Tommy's Dodge. They were so happy that they congratulated Tommy so much because they felt that the car was part theirs, and Tommy said, "It belongs to all of us."

Twenty-seven

After supper, Tommy drove to Ann's house. When Ann came to the door, Tommy said, "I have another surprise for you."

Ann replied, "Another surprise?"

Tommy said, "I finally bought that used Dodge that I have been talking about. I want to take you for a ride."

Ann said, "Let me get my jacket, and I'll be glad to go."

Since it was dark, Tommy had left the Dodge parked under the village light one hundred feet away.

Ann walked excitedly around the Dodge. She asked, "You mean this car is yours?"

Tommy laughed and said, "It really is mine. Bought and paid for with my mom's money."

Tommy held the door open on the passenger side. He said, "We'll have many rides in this Dodge in the next few years. I'm sure we'll always remember our first ride."

Ann said, "Where are we going?"

Tommy answered, "You name it."

Ann thought a minute and then said, "Let's go to Gilmore. I want to do a little shopping."

Tommy answered, "That's okay with me. Then we'll go to John's place for a soda."

Later they were parked at their favorite spot at the Gilmore Lake. Ann was in Tommy's arms as usual, when he said, "Let's check our future plans. I graduate from Illinois College this spring. If I get a job teaching chemistry and physics this fall, when do we get married?"

Ann answered, "I'm saving a little money. You'll have to save some money so we can buy our furniture."

Tommy said, "You are right as usual." Then he kissed Ann and said, "Maybe I better buy some condoms. I don't know if I can hold off that long?"

Ann kissed him and said, "We have held off this long, we should be able to hold off a little longer." Then she pulled herself out of Tommy's arms and said, "It isn't easy for me either. I love you so much. Let's go home."

Tommy said, "You are right." He started the Dodge and headed for Hinders.

Twenty-eight

Mike O'Neil was having the same trouble with Mary that Tommy was having with Ann. He couldn't keep his hands off of her.

Before Mike became serious with Mary, he was a frequent visitor to Maggie's Black Cat, taking care to always use a condom to protect him from venereal diseases and an unwanted pregnancy. He realized, of course, that a condom wasn't a perfect shield.

After Mary's ultimatum, no sex before marriage, Mike considered going back to Maggie's. He knew Maggie well enough to talk to her. She was always friendly. He dropped in one evening and told Maggie he was getting intimate with a lady in town.

Maggie laughed and said, "If we only depended on single men in our business, we would go broke."

After a beer, Mike said, "I'm sure you know your business very well. I'll wait and see how things develop." Then he departed.

The twins didn't need Tommy's '24 Dodge. They had the Victoris' new '28 Model A Ford. They weren't sure who was going to drive. Then Paul said, "You drove home from Carmount so I'll drive tonight. That means I'll pick up my girlfriend first. Then we'll pick up Mabel."

After they picked up the girls, Jimmy said, "Where to? Where do you want to go?"

Nancy, who was sitting in front with Paul, said, "Why don't we just ride around in this nice new car until eight o'clock and then we can go to Hamburg's and dance?"

"That sounds good to me," said Mabel.

"Paul, you are driving. We'll just sit back and relax," said Jimmy.

Paul said, "We'll drive around the Gilmore Lake and by then it'll be time to go to the dance."

When they arrived at Hamburg's, the dance was in full swing. They were already calling a barn dance. They stood on the side together until the dance was over and the next dance was a foxtrot. Jimmy grabbed Mabel and Paul paired off with Nancy.

Except for the barn dance, the twins danced with their own girlfriends most dances. Occasionally, the twins traded partners.

At intermission, they went to the liquor counter and the men drank beer and the ladies had soda. They sat down at a table and Nancy said, "Tell us about college. How are things going?"

Paul said, "School is getting to be routine. The second week was not routine. We had freshman initiation week, and the sophomores had all the fun."

Jimmy said, "Paul and I had to get the signature of two confessed virgins."

Paul said, "It would have been easy if I had been home. We could have taken our notebook and gotten your signatures."

The girls laughed, and Mabel said, "What did you do?"

Jimmy said, "We went over to the girls' dorm and started knocking on doors."

"What happened?" asked Nancy.

Paul said, "We started knocking on doors and had them slammed in our faces."

"Then we stopped at the lounge and explained our problem and got the two signatures. I'm sure that the girls didn't use their real names, but who cares, we had the signatures."

After the dance, Paul and Jimmy took their girl-friends directly home. The girls had strict curfews from their parents, and they knew if they did not get home shortly after the dance, midnight deadline, they would not be allowed out the following weekend.

Twenty-nine

Mike O'Neil was invited to the Victori home for Thanksgiving and Christmas. He had been spending the two holidays with the O'Neil family; his mother and dad were
still living. However, the O'Neils were getting up in age
and Mrs. O'Neil no longer had the big dinners for the
clan. The daughters had taken over and Mike had been
going to his sisters' homes.

They had to be given the full story of why Mike was
planning on spending the holidays with the Victoris.
Mike had to tell them that he had given Mary a ring,
and was engaged, and planned on a June wedding. The
O'Neils did not know whether to be happy or not, as Mike
was marrying a widow with four children. When Mike
explained that Tommy, the oldest, was a senior in college,
the twins were freshmen in college, and the youngest was
a freshman in high school, they realized that he was marrying into a family that believed in education. They were
happy that Mike had found true love and were eager to
meet Mary Victori and her family.

When Mike came to the Victori home for Thanksgiving, the family welcomed him. Mike was feeling at ease
with the children. Even Kay would give him a willing
kiss of welcome.

They ate the turkey and all the delicacies that Mary
had prepared and finished with the pumpkin pie. After
a couple of hours, the children all left, Tommy went to
Ann's, the twins went to their girlfriends', and Kay departed to visit a girlfriend.

Mary and Mike were left with the dishes and cleaning up. Mary said, "Mike, after you marry into this family, you'll be left with me and the work to do."

Mike said, "You and the children will be my reward, and I don't mind the work."

They sat down together on the divan in the living room. Mike told Mary how the O'Neils always spent the holidays with his mother and dad, how the sisters had taken over Thanksgiving and Christmas, and how eager the O'Neil clan was to meet Mary and her family.

"I wonder how we can arrange for the Victori family to meet the O'Neil clan?" asked Mike.

Mary, who was now in Mike's arms, asked, "Do the O'Neils have a family reunion?"

Mike answered, "We have a reunion every summer, but we have to get together before our wedding."

Mary said, "We could give a big engagement party at Hamburg's."

Mike said, "That sounds like a good idea but I wouldn't want you to go to a lot of trouble." After thinking a short time, Mike said, "Would you object if the O'Neil clan gave us an engagement party? We have the numbers."

Mary, after a hug and a kiss, said, "Talk it over with your family."

Mike immediately got up and said, "All the O'Neils are at my sister Colleen's house in Staunton today. That is less than ten miles from here. I would like to call Colleen and ask permission for me to bring you over, and they could all meet you. You are all dressed in that beautiful blue dress and should be ready to go."

Mary jumped up and said, "I wouldn't want to intrude."

Mike said, "Let me call."

Mary asked, "What about the kids?"

Mike said, "We'll call Tommy and Ann up first and see if they can come home and feed the family?"

Against her better judgment, with the urging of Mike, she called the Shinskis and talked to Tommy and Ann. When they heard of Mike and Mary's plans, they readily agreed and said that they would come right over.

In the meantime, Mike called his sister, Colleen, who told him, "Bring her right over. I think it is a wonderful idea."

As soon as Tommy and Ann arrived, after a few words of advice and instructions from Mary, Mike and Mary took off in Mike's Model T Ford to Staunton. Mary was apprehensive, not knowing how the O'Neil family would greet her. She realized as a widow with four children, she might not get too good of a welcome.

Mike introduced Mary to his mother and father. Big Mike, as his father was called, looked so much like his son that Mary was tempted to kiss him when he held out his hand. Mary did kiss his mother, Agnes. They were both very friendly and welcomed her into the family. Then Mary met the two sisters, their husbands, and their families. Mary had always heard that the Irish were a friendly, joyful people, and the O'Neil family certainly proved it to Mary.

They gave her a hearty welcome with drinks to their health and happiness. Mike and Mary finally sat down and Mary had a chance to look around. She knew that this was Colleen's house. *What did Mike say her married name was? Oberta, yes that's it.* She could see why the family was meeting here. This was a big two-story house with a large living room, dining room, kitchen and family room.

When Mike and Mary were invited to stay for supper, Mary wanted to say no, but Mike said yes for both of them. The adults ate first, and then the children. After the children had eaten, the twelve adults sat down at the dining room table for coffee. Mary noticed that the men usually had spiked coffee, a coffee and whiskey. The O'Neils were a happy bunch, and the whiskey made them an even happier clan.

After coffee, at the insistence of Mary, she and Mike departed. "Oh, my goodness," said Mary on the way home. "I wonder how my four will fit in with all those O'Neils?"

Mike said, "Mary, we are not going to live with them. We'll only see them occasionally."

Mary said, "I only have my sister, Ann, and her family in the United States, and we don't see them very often."

Before they went into the Victori home, Mike gave Mary a kiss and a hug and said, "Don't worry, Mary. It will all work out."

Thirty

It was the first of May, and Tommy was looking forward to graduation. He had spent nearly four school years at Illinois College. He remembered when he started as a freshman. The four years had seemed like an interminable length of time. He smiled when he looked back; it seem as though the time had gone quickly.

Mary and Tommy were planning a graduation dinner at Moore's Café with the Victoris, Mike O'Neil, and Mary's sister, Ann, her husband and the only two of Ann's five children that would be able to attend. That, with Ann Shinski, made eleven people in attendance. Tommy had made arrangements with Mr. Moore at the beginning of his senior year for the dinner.

Mike O'Neil called Mary on May second and said he had a serious matter to discuss with her. He sounded so serious over the phone that it worried her. That evening he came over right after supper and said, "We are going for a ride. I'm going to park on Eagan's Road, and don't worry about my getting fresh."

Mary never said a word, but she became apprehensive as he braked the Model T to a stop. Mike said, "I never told you, but before I became a motorman, I was mine manager at the Old Maggie Mine in Kollinson, evidently just after your husband left. I was there for several years, until I had trouble with the owner. He accused me of making a play for his wife, which wasn't true. Anyway, I quit and went to work at the Little Dog Mine and then came to Hinders."

Mary listened without comment. Mike went on, "The mine, Old Maggie that is, has a new owner that worked at the mine when I was manager. He came into some money and bought the mine and offered me my old job as manager at twice the salary I was making before. I sure would like to accept the job, but that means postponing our marriage, unless you would be willing to move to Kollinson. With your store and family, I realize that wouldn't be possible. I've been giving it a lot of thought, but I haven't come up with a solution."

Mary said, "I'm absolutely flabbergasted." Tears came to her eyes, and she turned her head away.

Mike tried to put his arm around her and she pulled away and said, "I wouldn't want you to marry me, and in your mind, continually blame me for keeping you from getting the big promotion."

Mike said, "Do you have any suggestions?"

Mary said, "Go ahead and take the job. We'll put an announcement in the Gilmore paper that the wedding has been postponed because you are taking the mine manager's job at Old Maggie in Kollinson." Then she added, "Take me home. I want to think about this situation."

Mike said, "I don't blame you. I've been in a state of mind since I received the offer."

Mike drove slowly back to the Victori store. Mary departed without the usual hugs and kisses. Kay was the only one home when Mary came in, in tears. Kay heard and saw her mother so distraught; she was sobbing. Kay immediately ran to her mother and screamed, "Mother! Mother! What is the matter?"

Mary finally acquired control of herself, put her arms around Kay and said, "I'm sorry, honey. I'll tell you in a minute. Mike and I are postponing our wedding. He has been offered a job as manager of the Old Maggie Mine in Kollinson at a large salary increase. He can't very well turn it down, and he knows I can't go with him since I have the store to take care of and a family to support."

Kay asked, "Why can't he just continue working as a motorman in Hinders?"

Mary answered, "He could, but I don't want him feeling for years like he could have been doing much better if he hadn't married into the Victori family."

Mary said, "I'll have to tell Tommy and the twins when they come home this weekend."

Tommy and the twins couldn't believe their ears when Mary told them why the June marriage had to be postponed. They, of course, sympathized with their mother, but could see why Mike wanted to accept the job as mine manager at Old Maggie Mine in Kollinson.

Thirty-one

Mary did not want Tommy to change his plans for his graduation party at Moore's Café, a week from the coming Saturday. She told the Victori children that she planned to invite Mike and was going with him in his new 1928 Model A Ford. Ann and the children could ride in the Victoris' Ford with Tommy. They were all going to wait in Hinders Saturday morning for Mary's sister and family, have a light lunch in Jacksonville, go to the graduation at three o'clock in the afternoon, and then celebrate at Moore's Café.

All the Victoris could talk about was the postponed wedding and Tommy's college graduation. Mary made arrangements with Mike to come over before the children left for Saturday night dates. She wanted them to see that he had not changed into an ogre. Mike did not let on. He was his usual jolly happy self. In fact, he may have pushed a little too hard. The children tried, but could not relate in his presence.

Tommy picked up Ann and told her about how and why his mother's wedding had to be postponed. Tommy said, "I don't know that we can blame anyone. Mother has assumed that Mike would continue to work as a motorman at the Hinders mine and come and live with her. He had been living at Ma Jones' Boarding House in Hinders. Now he plans to live in Kollinson during the week and in his old boarding house on weekends."

Ann said, "I hope our plans do not change."

Tommy answered, "Two school teachers still plan on getting married in June of 1929, providing I get a teaching job."

Ann said, "I hope there is not a second June marriage postponement."

Graduation Saturday was a beautiful sunny day in May. Three cars left Hinders and headed for Jacksonville. As planned, they ate lunch and then headed for the Illinois College campus.

The Favero family, Mary's sister, Ann's family, had never been to the Illinois College campus. As they walked around the campus, Tommy told them that they were on the grounds of the oldest college in Illinois, founded in 1828.

Tommy was the first one of the Victori family and their relatives to graduate from college. Mary was so proud that for a few hours she forgot her own troubles and was determined to enjoy Tommy's (or was it her) day. She finally decided that it was Tommy's day and the Victoris' day.

The Victori family was impressed by the caps and gowns of the graduates and the faculty. They applauded and applauded, but the joy of Mary Victori was saddened by the absence of Tommy's father, Marion.

Dinner at Moore's Café was supervised by Mr. Moore with his newest suit, biggest gold cuffs on his white shirt, and white shoes with matching spats. The celebration had ample wine, but the three drivers were only allowed one alcoholic drink because they were driving home after the dinner.

Thirty-two

On Monday morning, Tommy climbed into the cage with John Combs and started telling John about the wonderful time the family had at his graduation. Mr. Combs shook hands with Tommy and congratulated him. Praise from Mr. Combs was always appreciated.

As they climbed into the motor cart, Tommy looked around at the small overhead lights along the entry, miner's lamps, sending out a minimum of light, and he thought, *These are really brave men who are called coal miners. I'm afraid we do not give them the credit they deserve for producing electricity and keeping our homes and businesses warm.*

John said, "We are going to do a big survey today."

Tommy said, "When you use the word big, I'm all ears."

John laughed, "I'm using the word big in distance. We are going to survey most of the new North 22 entry of the mine. It will only be a quickie, rough determination of coal mined in the last thirty days."

Tommy said, "As you know, I consider all your surveying interesting."

John answered, "However, you are going to be a chemistry and physics teacher and end up as a lawyer."

Tommy said, "I admit I'm traveling an unusual path but one never knows if it is the right journey. The twins, Paul and Jimmy, are working at Carmount College in construction this summer for twenty five cents an hour. That is better than sitting at home."

Mike O'Neil moved some of his belongings to a boarding house in Kollinson and kept his best clothing for weekends at Hinders. He wanted to continue going with Mary on weekends. He had discussed the possibility with Mary, and she agreed. Mary disliked the idea of losing Mike, whom she loved so deeply. No one could take Marion's place in her life. She and Marion had so much in common, had had a wonderful married life, and he was the father of their four children. However, she had to face reality, life the way it was, not the way she wanted it to be.

Mike made arrangements with Ma Jones, the owner of the boarding house in Hinders, for staying on the weekends. Ma Jones was not happy about losing Mike, but he made her feel better when he agreed to pay almost as much for a weekend as when he was present all week.

Mike O'Neil was so busy the first week at his new job that he did not make it back to Hinders until the second week. He had phoned Mary every night. That helped, but it was not the same as having him visit several times a week.

When the O'Neils heard about Mike's new job and the postponement of the wedding, the two sisters and the two brothers weren't happy about it. Mike had almost married a couple of times many years ago, and at forty-six he was still a bachelor. Mike's two brothers phoned him, and when they found out he was going to stay in Kollinson the first weekend, they decided to go visit him. Mike was always glad to see his two brothers, but he wondered what was up.

They asked him about his job. He told them how he had his old job back at twice the money. They said, "Mike, you have always made good money. How much have you saved?"

Mike answered, "Some."

His brothers, Joe and Jack, took turns asking him questions.

Joe asked, "Have you broken up with Mary Victori?"

Mike replied, "No, we intend to go together on the weekends."

Jack said, "Do you think there is any chance you and Mary will ever marry?"

Mike answered, "Not in the near future. Mary has to have the store to support her family."

Joe then said, "In other words, the wedding is off."

Mike said, "Let's go to the tavern and have a few drinks. You can call your wives and tell them you are spending the night with me."

Joe said, "Our wives will not be happy."

When Mike arrived at Victoris' store the following Saturday, Mary welcomed him with open arms. Kay also smiled at him, as if she was glad to see him.

Mary and Mike had a lot to talk about. They decided to go to Luigi's in Gilmore for a good Italian dinner, and then come back to the Victori living room to visit. Mike said that he liked his job as mine manager, but it had a lot more headaches and responsibilities and longer hours. He said to Mary, "In the last analysis, I would have to admit it is the money."

Mary asked, "Why do you feel you need more money?"

Mike answered, "I want to have more for you and your family."

Mary said, "The store takes care of me and my family. What's more, Tommy will be on his own now that he has finished college. In three years, when the twins graduate, I'll have only Kay at home. So you see you don't need more money for me."

Mike replied, "Are you telling me to give up my mine manager's job?"

"Not exactly, Mike," added Mary.

"That's the way I see it," said Mike.

"The decision is yours," answered Mary.

From that moment on, for the next two hours until Kay came home, Mike and Mary did everything to show their love except engage in fornication. Mary felt with the postponing of their marriage it would be more foolish than ever to have sex with Mike, and he agreed. However, that did not stop Mike from making a trip to Maggie's Black Cat at midnight.

Thirty-three

Tommy filled out applications for chemistry and physics teaching jobs in all the high schools in Limbo and the neighboring counties. July came, and although he had had two interviews, he did not have a job. As August approached, he decided he better go see the coal mine superintendent, Mr. Powers, who had hired him as an assistant surveyor the last five summers.

Before he went to see Mr. Powers, he decided to talk to Mr. Combs. One day when they were at the bottom and Tommy was doing a survey, he stopped and approached Mr. Combs. He said, "You know Mr. Combs, it is August and I still do not have a teaching job."

Mr. Combs said, "I did not want to ask, but I figured if you had a teaching job, I would be one of the first persons to know."

Tommy said, "You are right. So you really figured that I was still looking."

Mr. Combs asked, "Do you have any contingent plans?"

Tommy said, "You must be a mind reader. I was going to ask you if I do not get a teaching job in the next two weeks, would it be alright if I were to ask Mr. Powers about continuing as your assistant?"

"It certainly would be," said Mr. Combs. "But I must warn you that I doubt that he would hire you full time."

Seeing that his answer disappointed Tommy, Mr. Combs hastily added, "It will do no harm to try."

The first week in August, Tommy received a call from Albert Roberts, principal of Carmount High School, stating that if Tommy did not have a job, he would like to see him. Tommy told him he was still waiting. Mr. Roberts said he would see him at seven o'clock that evening in the high school office.

Tommy told Mr. Roberts, "I'll be there."

Tommy was surprised to get a phone call from Mr. Roberts because he was one of the two principals he had interviewed and Mr. Roberts notified him that another applicant had been given the job.

That evening he was at the Carmount High School office before seven o'clock. Mr. Roberts invited him in immediately. He said to Tommy, "I owe you an explanation. I notified you that the chemistry and physics job was filled. However, after saying yes the candidate changed his mind to no. Therefore, we will have a vacancy."

Tommy smiled. "I must say that I'm glad to hear that."

Mr. Roberts said, "I know I interviewed you, and I've rechecked your transcripts. I'm impressed with your scholarship. I'll tell you frankly, if you want the job for a salary of twelve hundred and fifty dollars for the school year, it's yours. The Board of Education will have to approve it, but I assure you that it is only part of the law in Illinois. The Board of Education does the hiring I recommend."

Tommy said, "I don't know what to say except I thank you, and I accept."

Tommy and Mr. Roberts shook hands, and Mr. Roberts handed Tommy a booklet telling about teaching in Carmount High School, "Rules and Regulations."

Then he said to Tommy, "You'll want to see the chemistry and physics laboratory and instruction rooms before you leave."

Tommy said, "I sure do. I'll also like to have a copy of the books and laboratory manuals and your equipment and supply inventories as soon as I can. I'll want to order what I need, with your approval of course."

Tommy went with Mr. Roberts upstairs and saw the standard old-type chemistry tables with shelving drawers and compartments for equipment. They seemed to be in good shape. The lecture room had ample board space and thirty chairs.

He told Mr. Roberts, "This will be fine. I wish I was going to start teaching Monday."

Mr. Roberts laughed and said, "School is less than a month away."

Tommy said, "I'll be back to check everything."

They went back to the office and Tommy shook hands again and thanked him vehemently.

Tommy hurried home to tell his mother and Ann, the twins, and Kay. Mary was so happy for Tommy that she kissed and hugged him repeatedly.

Tommy did not sit down with his mother very long, when he departed and quickly hurried over to Ann's house. Tommy had called Ann and told her the good news. She was waiting for him and came running out. She put her arms around Tommy and started screaming.

They sat on the swing and at the same time cried, "Now we can get married next June." They laughed and laughed.

Ann said, "Tell me about the job."

Tommy said, "I'm going to teach chemistry and physics for nine months for twelve hundred and fifty dollars per school year."

Ann said, "I'm going to make one hundred dollars a month for nine months this year. We are more fortunate than most of our friends."

Tommy said, "If I'm rehired next year, we'll probably live in Carmount."

Ann said, "That does not worry me."

"Nor me," said Tommy.

Thirty-four

It was the middle of August when Mary got a call from Colleen, Mike's sister. She was in tears. She said, "There has been an accident at the Old Maggie Mine. Mike had his left leg crushed, and he is calling for you."

Mary said, "Fortunately, Tommy is home, and I'll have him drive me to Kollinson. We know our way around the town. Remember, we lived there for years, and my sister, Ann, still lives there."

Colleen cried out, "He is at St. Mary's Hospital."

Mary answered, "We'll leave in a half an hour."

Mary told Tommy, "We better pack suitcases. We may have to stay at Ann's overnight."

Tommy covered the thirty miles in the new Victori Model A Ford in forty minutes and pulled up at St. Mary's Hospital. The O'Neils were in tears.

The brothers, Joe and Jack, said, "It happened in the mine. The ceiling fell and crushed his leg so badly that they are going to take it off."

"Oh my God, I hope not," cried Mary.

The sisters said, "Mike says he would rather die than lose a leg."

Joe in tears said, "I understand it's below the knee. That will make him mobile."

Jack said, "Thank God you were able to get here. He has been begging for you."

Tommy waited while the sisters took Mary into Mike's room. Mike was in a lot of pain, in spite of the morphine. He tried to smile when he saw Mary. He put his arms up, and Mary hugged him through their tears.

The Maggie Mine owner brought in a specialist from St. Louis, who after a careful examination said, "We may be able to save the leg. We'll certainly try."

The doctor then said, "There is nothing the family can do except pray. The doctors and nurses will do their best."

After Mary came out of Mike's room, Mary told the O'Neils that she and Tommy would stay overnight at her sister Ann's house and that they would return in the morning.

The O'Neils hugged Mary and thanked her and Tommy.

Ann and her husband were glad to see Mary and Tommy but felt badly about what happened to make the trip necessary. Ben Favero, Ann's husband, said, "I'm sure Ann can take care of all of us for supper. We only have our youngest, William—Bill—at home. The house is nearly empty."

Mary told the Faveros about Mike's accident and how the doctors were trying to save his leg. Before supper, they all joined in prayer for Mike O'Neil.

After supper they all sat around and talked. Tommy finally got around to telling his relatives about his new job as a chemistry and physics teacher at Carmount High School. After all the others had gone to bed, Ann talked person-to-person with her sister, Mary. Ann asked, "Are you going to marry Mike O'Neil?"

Mary answered, "I hope so. I really love him."

Ann again asked a second question. "What if he loses his leg?"

Mary again answered, "I'll still marry him."

Ann said, "You must take into account that he will not be able to work in the mine, and if he gets a disability pension, it won't be much."

Mary answered, "I've thought of that. If he can't get another job, he can work in the store."

Ann said, "Mary, you know as well as I do that Mike would not marry you if you had to support him. He is a proud Irishman and would never agree to marry you under those circumstances."

Mary, who had cried numerous times after she had heard of Mike's accident, shed more tears.

Ann came closer to Mary, put her arms around her and cried with her. She said, "Sis, you have had a rough time since Marion passed, struggling to make a living for your family. You have shown real courage. How you did it, I don't know. I'm not sure how you will overcome your latest problem, but I know you will. Let's go to bed and try to get some sleep."

The next morning was Saturday. Mary had called Kay and the twins and told them to take care of the store and Tommy and she would get home later that afternoon or Sunday.

After breakfast, they went back to St. Mary's Hospital. The O'Neils were at the hospital early. Putting their heads together and realizing that this would be a long vigil, they decided to work in shifts. Since Jack and Joe lived in Kollinson and worked at the old Maggie Mine, the sisters would stay with them.

When Mary and Tommy arrived, the O'Neils were just getting ready to leave, except for the one who drew the first shift. They greeted Mary and Tommy warmly and said there had been no changes. After viewing the x-ray and the other tests taken, the doctors were more hopeful, but they would wait until Monday morning to make their final decision.

Mary and Tommy went in but Mike was sleeping. The injured leg was uncovered, and they saw tubes protruding from it. It looked terribly discolored. They only stayed for a few minutes and went out to the waiting room.

Colleen, who was on duty, told Mary and Tommy that they appreciated their coming to Mike's bedside, but they realized that Mary had a store and family to take care of and did not expect them to stay.

Mary said after talking to Tommy, "We will leave after lunch at the hospital lunch room."

When Mike awakened for a short while in the middle of the morning he was coherent enough for Mary to talk to him.

She said, "Mike, the doctors are hopeful that they can save your leg."

Mike, with tears in his eyes, said, "God, I hope so."

Mary said, with tears in her eyes, very emphatically, "I know one thing. You big wonderful Irishman, you are going to marry me regardless of what happens."

Colleen, who had gone in with Mary, was bending over Mike's bed and squeezed her shoulders.

Thirty-five

After making one more trip to Mike's room, Tommy and Mary went to lunch and then departed for Hinders. When they went over the crossing at Hinders, they felt they were home. When Mary saw Kay and the twins waiting on customers, she realized that the people were being well taken care of.

Mary told the family, "We'll have supper together tonight."

At supper Mary explained to the twins and Kay why they were gone so long.

Kay asked, "They do not know if Mike is going to lose his leg?"

Tommy cut in and said, "Even the doctors are not sure. The specialist from St. Louis was the most encouraging. He told us to go home and pray. Mother and I have said many prayers."

After supper, Tommy got in his Dodge and headed for Ann's. The twins got in the Ford and went to pick up their girlfriends. Only Kay stayed home with their mother. Mary sat at the table with her coffee as if in a trance.

Kay asked, "What are you thinking, Mother?"

Mary turned her head toward Kay and said, "Honey, I'm at a loss. One minute I think they will save Mike's leg and in a few months he'll be back to work. The next minute, I see Mike with only one leg, and I'm afraid he won't be able to do any job in the mine, and he won't marry me because he'll only be a handyman in the Victori store."

Kay held her mother's hand and said, "At fifteen years of age I can't give you much advice, but I know one thing, Mother, worrying will not help."

Mary answered, "You are right. I'll try to be as optimistic as I can be, but I'll be glad when I know, yes or no, about the operation."

Kay said, "I'll add my prayers to yours."

Mary said, "Thank you, dear."

Tommy told Ann about Mike O'Neil's problem. Ann was very sympathetic.

The twin's girlfriends also expressed their sympathy. However, they all realized that they were not going to be of much help and life would go on.

They all went to the theatre and then went out to a late snack.

Monday morning Mary and Kay were waiting on customers in the Victori store when the phone rang. This time it was Colleen with good news. The specialist said that with a couple operations, he felt sure he could save Mike's leg.

Mary, all smiles, gave the good news to Kay.

Kay asked, "When are you going to see Mike again?"

Mary said, "Tommy has already been to St. Mary's Hospital, so I'll have the twins take me this evening, and you can go along too if you want to."

Kay said, "I want to."

When Mary, the twins, and Kay met the O'Neils that were present, Mary said, "You met Tommy who was here with me over the weekend. These are the twins, Jimmy and Paul, and my daughter, Kay."

Jack who seemed to be in charge said, "Mike is feeling a little better. Mary, go in first and if Mike is up to it, you can call the children in to say hello."

101

Mary went into Mike's room. Mike was expecting her. She bent over hugged and kissed him. Mike did his best to smile. He was still heavily sedated. When Mary told him about the kids, Mike said, "Bring them in."

The Victori children shook hands with Mike and stood around smiling at him.

Mike said, "All of you are welcome."

After a couple minutes, they quickly went back to the waiting room. After a few minutes more Mary also came to the waiting room.

The O'Neils said, "Mike will have his first operation on his leg tomorrow. The next operation will depend on how the first one comes out."

Mary said, "While we are in Kollinson, we will make a brief visit to the Faveros, my sister's family."

Mary, the twins, and Kay made a brief trip to her relatives. They had drinks and eats, thanked Ann, and then headed back to Hinders.

Thirty-six

Mike O'Neil's first operation led to a second. After a month in St. Mary's Hospital, he went to his sister Colleen's home to recuperate. Staunton was only eight miles from Hinders. Thus, Mary was able to visit Mike often.

Tommy started teaching chemistry and physics in Carmount High School and the twins were sophomores in Carmount College, while Kay was in second year of high school in Gilmore.

Mary and Mike were planning a fall wedding so they would not interfere with Tommy and Ann's wedding in June.

From the first day in class in September, Tommy enjoyed teaching chemistry and physics. His classes were all electives. The students were in his classes because they chose to be. He remembered his first lecture to his classes. Although the subjects were different, he told them the same thing. "Very few of you will become scientists. You will learn the basics of chemistry and physics in my classes and that is important. However, more important, is learning the scientific method, a way of thinking, of problem solving. The general rules used today were worked out by many men and women during hundreds of years of trial and error.

"The scientific method has five check points, which I'm going to explain to you. When I'm done some of you will think as I used to say when I was your age when something was not clear, 'It sounds like pig Latin to me.' However, don't worry about that. We will review these points over and over as we do scores of experiments in our laboratory work."

Tommy went over the five check points:

1. Recognizing and stating the problem.
2. Hypothesis, coming up with a possible explanation.
3. Experimentation and observation.
4. Collecting and interpreting data.
5. Drawing conclusions.

He finished by saying, "A scientist never accepts a conclusion because it is what he wants to happen, but rather what the results of the scientific method are."

The second week the students did their laboratory work in pairs under Tommy's watchful eyes. He did not want anyone to get burned or injured. Tommy had spent one of the laboratory double periods showing the students the use of the protective aprons and goggles in the chemistry class as well as the Bunsen burners, test tube holders, and other equipment.

When Ann started teaching first grade, she was always telling Tommy about some of the things that happened in school. Now it was his turn.

They laughed at each other's stories. Since they were both teachers, they had a lot of things in common, including work days and days off such as Saturdays and Sundays, holidays and summers.

They still enjoyed most evenings and weekends together. Although, they taught in different towns, they attended the same teacher institutes. In mid-October on Thursday, they had the county institute in Carmount. Since they lived in Hinders, they started together, spent the day together, and went home together. Tommy did the driving and used his Dodge. In Carmount, they had lunch at Taylor's Chili Parlor. Taylor's made their own chili, mild or strong. The chili was tasty.

On Friday, Tommy and Ann attended the institute at the theater in Springfield. After the institute, Tommy and Ann went to see Lincoln's Tomb at the Oak Ridge Cemetery. Thousands of people visit his tomb each year. Tommy and Ann read his farewell address in Springfield. He said, "Here I have lived a quarter of a century and I have passed from a young to an old man."

Tommy couldn't help but wonder at that moment. At the time, Lincoln was fifty-two years old and later died from a shot by John Wilkes Booth at the Ford's Theater in Washington, D.C. at the age of fifty-six. Tommy and Ann realized the term old was relative and in the days of Abraham Lincoln fifty years was considered old.

Tommy and Ann were impressed by Lincoln from an early childhood through grade school, high school, and college. Now that they were teachers, they were more impressed than ever by how a man who was born in a log cabin with a very limited education could become the President of the United States and have the courage and ability to save the Union.

The most startling statement was made by one of the speakers when he said, "I was amazed to learn that black people could not rent a room overnight at the Lincoln Hotel."

Thirty-seven

Mike O'Neil was recovering rapidly. It had been two months since his accident and he had put away his crutches, and only walked with a slight limp as he walked through Hinders in the beautiful October weather.

The last two months, one in St. Mary's Hospital and one at his sister Colleen's, in Staunton, had gone slowly. Now he had moved back to Ma Jones' Boarding House in Hinders where he had friends he could visit with.

Mike's biggest pleasure was his short two block walk to the Victori store where he could visit with Mary, Kay and Tommy, as well as Paul and Jimmy when they were home. If Kay or one of the other children were around to watch the store, Mary would go for a walk with Mike, and today was a special day. The twins were home. They were going to help Mike climb the Hinders hill. Then Mike and Mary were going to take an hour sitting on the edge of the hill and watch the birds, fishermen, and swimmers. At the end of the hour, Paul and Jimmy were going to help Mike down the hill, and then Mary was going to walk Mike back to the boarding house.

Mike and Mary sat on a log overlooking the Hinders pond. They were both all smiles. This was indeed a treat for both of them. Now they could understand why Tommy and Ann told them about how enjoyable this particular view was.

Mary asked, "You have definitely made up your mind to come back to Hinders as a motorman?"

Mike said, "I not only made up my mind, I have cleared it with my old boss and the mine manager."

Mary threw her arms around Mike and gave him a kiss. Then she said, "I'll do my best to make you happy. I hope you'll never regret giving up your job as mine manager."

They were like two kids, holding hands and enjoying themselves. Mike's injury and suffering during his period in the hospital had shown him how important family was. The O'Neil family had been magnificent and yet it wasn't enough. Mike knew why. With all the O'Neils around him, each with their own family, he felt like an outsider. That's why in his moments of his greatest suffering, he called for Mary. He too had to have his own family. As they sat there, happy in each other's company, Mike explained all these feelings to Mary.

Mary understood perfectly well what Mike was talking about. Not very long ago when she saw Tommy, the twins, and then Kay growing up and leaving her, she realized how important Mike would be to her. They would always be her children and they would always love each other, but each of them would have their own families. Thus, she needed Mike, whom she loved.

They looked forward to their marriage in the fall. Mary had two marriages to look forward to, Tommy and Ann's in the spring came first. She would help, but she realized that Ann and the Shinskis would handle it. Her participation would be minimal.

They heard voices behind them. They looked back and there were the twins. In unison they said, "Don't tell me that the hour is up?"

Jimmy and Paul laughed and Paul said, "We were told to be here in one hour."

Paul added, "The hour is up."

Mike put out a hand and Jimmy helped him get off the log. Paul got on the other side and Mike said, "Now that you have me up, I'll walk to the edge of the hill. Then you can help me down the hill and over the tracks."

When they reached the Victori building they went in the back door, and Mary said to Mike, "Sit down and I'll get you a cold beer."

Mike said, "That sounds great to me."

A half an hour later, Mary walked Mike back to Ma Jones' Boarding House.

Mary said, "Mike, you sure did well today. When do you think you will be able to go back to work in the mine?"

Mike gave Mary a kiss and said, "I hope to go back in another month."

Mary had just left when Julius Ersp, the mine manager, came in. He asked Mike, "How are you doing?"

Mike answered, "Better every day."

Julius said, "That's good. I have a new proposition to make you. You are an experienced mine manager. How would you like to be my assistant?"

Mike just sat there. He could not believe his ears. Then he said, "You have got to be kidding."

"No, I am not," said Julius. "The job is yours."

Mike said, "Please come here, I want to shake your hand and thank you."

Mike had to call Mary and tell her about the new job as assistant mine manager.

Mary was thrilled because she felt badly about Mike giving up his job as mine manager to come to Hinders to work as a motorman again. Now she knew that eventually Mike would be a mine manager again.

Thirty-eight

Tommy and Jack Wenz had started night school at Lincoln Law School in Springfield. They had made arrangements to catch the Illinois Terminal at Gilmore at six o'clock in the evening, and arrive in Springfield in forty-five minutes. They would be in class by seven o'clock. After a couple of weeks, they realized that this would not work too well. They had met two other students from Litchfield, Leo Macy and Oscar Fell, one a school teacher and the other a banker, who were driving from Litchfield so they decided they would meet at Litchfield and take turns driving, a distance of about forty-five miles. Tommy and Jack drove together to Litchfield and rode to Springfield with whoever's turn it was to drive. This worked much better than using the train.

They went three nights a week from seven to ten o'clock in the evening. All but the driver, when weather permitted, would read law cases and subject matter that they would listen to and discuss, which helped considerably as they were always pressed for time.

They also were pressed for time to eat at home and pressed for money to eat on the road. There were times when they didn't have ten dollars among the four of them. They would stop at a tavern that had free eats with their drinks, and thus satiate their hunger on the cheap.

Tommy and Jack became good friends with Leo and Oscar. They rode together and studied together on the road, at school, and at the various homes. They did a lot of studying on the weekends and at night when they had no classes, especially before semester examinations.

109

Tommy, who was also still in his first year of teaching and had to work out a program and prepare equipment and supplies, found that he had less time for Ann. They saw each other as often they could, but Tommy rarely stayed late. Ann understood and helped Tommy all she could. She even read law with him and realized that more and more women were going to law school. Limbo County had had one woman lawyer for the last twenty years. Now she heard there were half a dozen women from the county in law school.

Tommy and Ann set June ninth as their wedding date. Since she and Tommy had summers off, they planned a honeymoon in the mountains of Colorado. It happened that a classmate of Ann's was teaching in Denver, and they planned to spend a night with her newly married friend and her husband.

The twins, Paul and Jimmy, were graduating from Carmount Junior College and had already enrolled at the University of Illinois for their junior year. They both wanted to become civil engineers and they knew Illinois had a good program. They both had applied at the State of Illinois for the State Summer Program on the Illinois highways, an eight-week program, and they were both fortunate enough to be accepted.

Tommy had made arrangements to work in the law office of the state's attorney for the summer, after he returned from his honeymoon.

Mary and Kay continued to work in the Victori Country Store. They were busy but enjoyed their work and were happy doing what they were doing.

Mike and Mary decided to add a bedroom to the Victori building and make it as modern as Hinders' conditions permitted. They had to have a well and cistern, a basement for a furnace, stool, sink, tub, shower, and bathroom, pipes for hot air, plumbing, pumps, and a septic tank. Fortunately, Mike had saved some money and they borrowed the rest. The Victori building was one of the few living quarters with those conveniences.

Thirty-nine

Tommy Victori and Ann Shinski were married on June 9, 1929 at the Catholic Church in Gilmore. Ann looked beautiful in her white wedding gown. Standing beside her, all dressed in blue were her maid of honor, Mary Bruno, and the bridesmaids, the twins' girlfriends, Mabel Re and Nancy Down, and Tommy's sister, Kay. The men, all lined up in tuxedos, were Tommy, Harry Shinski, Ann's brother and the best man, the twins, Paul and Jimmy, and Dean Basse, Tommy's good friend.

The organist played the "Wedding March," and Ann came in on the arm of her father, Mr. Shinski, who gave her away. The reception was held at the Gilmore Country Club with Sie's Band playing many of the romantic songs of the '20s.

After the dance, Tommy and Ann got in the Victoris' Model A Ford and headed for the Ozarks, over two hundred miles away. However, they had reservations the first night at the Stardust Inn about twenty miles from Gilmore.

Tommy drove Ann to the Shinski home and waited for her to change out of her wedding gown and put on a skirt and blouse to travel. Her suitcase was already packed. Tommy didn't have to stop as his suitcase was already in the trunk. While he was waiting for Ann, he took off his tie and jacket and tried to relax. When Ann came out with her suitcase, he put it on top of his in the trunk.

Less than an hour later, they checked in at the Stardust Inn and hurried to their room on the first floor.

Tommy took Ann in his arms and they helped each other take off their clothes. There was no air conditioner and they were perspiring profusely. Tommy said to Ann, "I'll be gentle." They spent the next hour making love. Exhausted they finally went to sleep.

Forty

When Tommy and Ann were on their honeymoon, Mike O'Neil told Mary, "I want to be completely honest with you. I have a confession to make to the woman I want to marry. When I came to work at the Hinders mine, I knew very few people in Hinders. I moved into Ma Jones' Boarding House. She runs a strict clean place with good food and good service. However, as you can appreciate, the boarders were, and are, single men looking for a place to live.

"I'm not making excuses, but they introduced me to the houses of prostitution in town. I settled on the Maggie's Black Cat and visited it periodically. After I started going with you, I stopped going to the Black Cat. I've only been there one time since and that was the night you told me there would be no sex until we married. I've regretted that ever since. I wanted you to know all this and the fact that I have taken a complete physical examination because I wanted to be sure I did not give you any social diseases."

He stopped talking and looked at Mary.

Mary smiled and put her arms around Mike, and she told him, "Michael, I've been married and have four children. I know and understand men. Your honesty and frankness are commendable. I really appreciate your telling me. I want to tell you that I did not think that a man forty-six would be a virgin.

"Let's go out to supper, and if your needs are so great that you can't wait until we get married in October, we'll make love before then."

Mike grabbed Mary and hugged and kissed her. Then he said, "What a wonderful woman!"

Forty-one

When Tommy and Ann reached Denver, they checked in at the Gold Nugget Hotel, and Ann called her friend, Rose Bentley, now Rose Handy. They made arrangements to meet at the Gold Nugget Hotel and let the Handy friends select a place to eat, since they were well acquainted with Denver.

They met in the lobby of the hotel and Ann introduced Tommy as her friend, then blushing, she said, "And husband."

Rose introduced her husband, Frank Handy. They sat down and talked for half an hour and Rose showed them pictures of their wedding. Ann said, "We won't see our pictures until we get back."

They then got in Frank's car and he said, "We'll take you to Tony's. It is as good an Italian restaurant as any in Denver, and I figured that Tommy, with a name like Victori, would appreciate good Italian food."

Tommy said, "You are correct, both Ann and I like good Italian food."

Ann and Rose has a lot of catching up to do and were conversing with each other most of the time. Tommy turned to Frank and said, "You are having supper with three teachers. I know you don't want to hear three teachers talk shop. What do you do to earn a living?"

Frank said, "I'm an architect and as the sun sets I'll drive you around town to show you our beautiful downtown Denver. As you know Denver is the capital city of Colorado, and we'll show you our beautiful golden dome capitol building."

116

"That sounds good to me," said Tommy.

As they finished their desserts, Tommy said, "Frank, tell the girls what your plans are."

They went to the restaurant parking lot, got into Frank's new 1928 Dodge, and started their sightseeing. Frank said, "Although we don't have the money to build yet, we have bought a lot, and I want to take you by there tomorrow. I'm sure you'll like the view overlooking the South Platte River ten miles east of the Rocky Mountains."

When they were done with their sightseeing Frank said, "Now I'll take you to a night spot, and we can have an illegal drink. There is plenty of booze in Denver, or if you prefer, you can have a Coke."

Tommy and Ann spent a couple of days in Denver, then headed south sixty-five miles to the best known of the Rocky Mountain peaks in Colorado, Pike's Peak. It lifts its snowcapped peak 14,110 feet above sea level. Tommy and Ann took the thirty-mile auto trip from Colorado Springs with a professional driver. As they went up and up, stopping at road views, and then looking down and around through telescopes, the scenery was magnificent.

Tommy and Ann returned through the wheat fields of Kansas then to Springfield, Missouri and the Shepard of the Hills Country, where Harold Bell Wright lived when he wrote the book by the same name in 1907. The Victoris enjoyed the Shepard of the Hills play, stayed overnight in Branson, and headed for Illinois and Hinders the next day.

As they went by the Hinders pond, the hill, and the North Railroad they couldn't help contrast the beautiful mountains of Colorado with their trees and snowcaps to the Hinders where they grew up, fell in love, were back visiting until they went to their furnished apartment in Carmount.

The Victoris, the Shinskis, and Mike O'Neil welcomed them home. They had all agreed to have supper at the Victori store where they would set up tables and chairs and there would be room for everyone.

Mary Victori and Agnes, Ann's mother, had agreed on a menu, and they both prepared a share. Thus, there was ample food and dishes that everyone liked. Red wine was plentiful, but Tommy drank only one glass because he and Ann had to go to Carmount after supper, and they wanted to reach their new home safely.

Forty-two

Tommy went to work in the State's Attorney Ed Feld's office on Monday after he returned from his honeymoon. Ed made it a point to say hello and welcomed Tommy to his office. Everyone was friendly. Lawyers and secretaries treated him well.

A couple of the lawyers asked him how he enjoyed his honeymoon with a knowing wink. Tommy ignored the winks and talked about Colorado, Denver, and Pike's Peak. He promised to show them the pictures they had taken as soon as they were developed.

Tommy had attended Lincoln Law School for one year and was familiar with the terminology and the general cases and procedures in a law office. However, he had a limited knowledge of the work that went on in the State's Attorney's Office, particularly how the elected official prepared cases for the State and represented it in court. Tommy knew that the State's Attorney had a lot of criminal cases.

One of the Assistant State's Attorneys was appointed as his mentor. Andy Pike, the mentor, had a book about the duties and the Office of the State's Attorney. Andy gave Tommy a run down and briefs on the cases the State's Attorney's Office had handled in the present year, 1929.

After a couple of hours of assistance each day for a week, Andy said to Tommy, "Now, I'm going to put you on your own. As you read and observe in our office and in court if you have any questions come to me and I'll try to help."

Tommy answered and said, "Andy, you and everyone in your office has been so friendly and helpful that I know I'm going to enjoy my summer here."

Tommy read about the criminal cases on the docket for the summer. The legal proceeding that caught his eye was the case of a sixteen-year-old girl who, with her family, had gone to a wedding in Gilmore as a bridesmaid to a cousin. That evening at the reception she had given her father a ride to the Gilmore Lake, where they were staying with the bride's father and mother. However, on the way back to the reception, in the lake area, a car with a red flasher had pulled her aside and kidnapped her. She was found dead in a cornfield near a neighboring town several days later. The murderers, two men, had been caught, convicted, and sentenced to death. They were on death row for years and then were taken off of death row and given a life sentence by an Illinois governor.

Tommy went home to his apartment each evening and told Ann how interesting his summer work was. Ann was busy taking courses toward her degree. She had gone into teaching with the elementary certificate she received after two years in college. Thus, her desire was to eventually get a degree. She had been taking extension courses from Illinois State Normal and courses available at Carmount College to get her degree in education from Normal.

At least one night a week they went to Hinders to visit the Victori family and the Shinski family. They found that the Victori family was getting ready for Mary's wedding to Mike O'Neil in October.

Mike had started his new job as assistant mine manager. Mike found out why Julius Erps needed an assistant. The mine hired five hundred men and was getting larger as it helped supply the needs of the North Railroad and the electricity produced by the new generating plants in an expanding and growing Illinois.

Mary Victori's and Michael O'Neil's wedding was to be a very private affair. Those attending from Mary's side were the Victori family and her sister, Ann, and her family. Those attending from the O'Neil family were Mike's father and mother, Mike's two sisters and their families, and Mike's two brothers and their families.

The couple was married at the Catholic Church in Gilmore, and the reception was held at the Knights of Columbus Hall, near the church, right after the wedding. The Victori and O'Neil families enjoyed the dinner and reception, which gave them a good opportunity to become better acquainted.

Mike O'Neil and Mary Victori, now Mr. and Mrs. Michael O'Neil, went on a short honeymoon trip to the Abraham Lincoln Hotel in Springfield for a few days. They checked in the hotel, went to their room, and enjoyed their love and sexual freedom. They both felt as happy as only newlyweds can experience.

Mike said, "My family wondered if I would ever get married. I never let on, but I had really given up myself. My lady selection had never worked until you came along. I'm glad I waited for the right woman."

Mary said, "I never thought I could be happy again, but you proved that I was wrong."

Mike added, "You know I'm hungry. Why don't we celebrate at the hotel restaurant and then we can come upstairs and celebrate some more."

Mary laughed and said, "You know I think this marriage is going to be a big success."

Forty-three

The year 1929 was coming to an end, and the Victori family and the Shinski family found out that Ann was pregnant and expecting a baby in June. Tommy and Ann were hoping it would be born on June 9, their first anniversary, but Kara came on June 10, 1930.

The Victoris and the Shinskis were overjoyed. In addition to Ann's mother, Grandma Agnes, and father, Grandpa Steve, there was Uncle Harry, the twins, Uncles Jimmy and Paul, Aunt Kay, and Grandma Mary O'Neil. Kara had so many people wanting to take care of her that she was never alone except when she was sleeping, and even then there was always someone close by.

However, in pure bliss, no one could compare with Ann and Tommy, who saw in Kara resemblances that others could not see. The nose like Ann's, the eyes like Tommy's, the shape of the forehead and chin like different family members. Parenthood was wonderful.

Ann kept a baby book and she and Tommy were always taking pictures. The least little whimper at night and they were both up. After a few weeks of getting little sleep, they were tired. There was no school the next day and Ann tried to catch up on her sleep but Tommy had to report to the State's Attorney's Office. Grandma Mary, who had raised four children, told Tommy that they should take turns getting up until the baby became older and would sleep longer.

They received a baby bed, baby buggy, and play pen as well as numerous other presents. The apartment was getting too small, so Tommy and Ann started to look for a house to buy in Carmount.

They found a three bedroom house with a kitchen, dining room, living room, full basement, and garage for five thousand dollars. They had both received a small raise in their teacher salaries. They made arrangements with the local bank to borrow four thousand dollars and bought the house.

Then came the need for furniture. They got help from the Victori-O'Neil family and the Shinski family including some furniture that they no longer needed, and some secondhand furniture. They bought all the new furniture that they could afford. They had to be careful that their house and furniture payments stayed within their budget. Tommy remarked, "We'll keep my 1924 Dodge as long as it runs."

When school started, they had to hire a babysitter, and Ann drove Tommy to the Carmount High School and then drove the six miles to Gilmore Elementary School.

They had had Thanksgiving with the Shinski family and were planning Christmas with the Victori family. Even though Kara would only be a little over six months old for Christmas, Tommy and Ann cut a tree near Hinders and decorated it and had one string of lights.

Kara, the baby, was the center of attention. They all realized that the future Christmases, two, three, four, five and six and so on, would be the ones Kara would understand and she could express her thoughts through words.

All the Victoris tried not to show it, but there were times when Marion was on their minds. Life goes on, however, and they were happy to celebrate together.

Time was flying by. Tommy was in his third year of law school. He and Jack Wenz, Leo Macy, and Oscar Fell were still driving to Lincoln Law School three nights a week. At times, the weather was bad, but they usually made it to Springfield.

More than ever, they said, "We must finish law school or we will have wasted a lot of time, effort and money for nothing."

Jimmy and Paul were in their last year of the civil engineering program at Illinois and looking forward to graduating and going to work the year around for the State of Illinois, which was building more and more roads and bridges as they were finding out during their summer work.

Kay, four years behind the twins, was graduating from high school and was looking forward to attending the University of Illinois. She had changed her mind several times about her future plans and wasn't sure what her vocation would be.

Ann, Mary Victori, and Agnes Shinski continued dressing Kara like a beautiful doll. Kara was getting a little spoiled but the only ones that noticed were her parents, particularly Ann who spent so much time with her.

The first graduation was Kay's, the last Friday of May, followed by the twins, Paul and Jimmy, the next afternoon on Saturday in Champaign. The Victoris watched Kay get her high school diploma. Mary couldn't believe that the last of her four children had finished high school.

Harry Barnes, a freshman at Illinois, was there to see Kay and shake her hand in congratulations. They had gone with each other sporadically during the last four years and were still very much interested in each other. The Victoris were having a graduation party at the store and Harry was invited.

Tommy and Ann decided to bring Kara and let her participate for a little while. The decorations, including red bells and white and blue crepe paper, caught her eye, and Tommy let her hold one of the red bells. She was smiles when they let her taste a few teaspoons of ice cream.

Kay kept her cap and gown on until pictures of the group could be taken. One of the first pictures was that of Kara being held by her Aunt Kay.

It was a relaxing evening to be followed by a trip to Champaign on Saturday. They went in two 1928 Model A Fords. One was driven by Mike O'Neil and the other by Tommy Victori. Among the hundreds receiving degrees in engineering, there were only two sets of twins, including Paul and Jimmy.

Paul had broken up with Nancy and Jimmy with Mabel, and the twins were now playing the field. They went for pictures and dinner at the Urbana Hotel where they were staying overnight. The following morning, they ate a late breakfast and headed for Limbo County.

In Hinders, Mary and Kay took care of the store which had been handled by the two women that filled in when either Mary or Kay was absent and Mike was back at his job as assistant mine manager of the Hinders mine. In Carmount, Ann was looking after Kara and Tommy was back at the State's Attorney's Office.

The twins were taking a week's vacation in Colorado, listening to suggestions by Tommy and Ann that they should take in the beautiful Rocky Mountain scenery before reporting to their jobs as civil engineers in Springfield and the level land of Illinois.

Forty-four

Illinois was enjoying the beautiful blue skies of June when Ann noticed that Kara was coming down with a cold. It seemed to be getting worse, and Ann took Kara to Dr. Ed Wester, her physician. He gave Ann medicine to give Kara.

However, the medicine didn't seem to help, and Kara was having trouble breathing. Dr. Wester came to the house, checked Kara, and told Ann and Tommy to take the child to the local hospital and that his diagnosis was pneumonia. Tommy and Ann took Kara to the hospital and then called the Victori and Shinski families. It was the ninth of June and the grandparents had already bought Kara's birthday presents since the next day, June 10, was Kara's birthday.

The hospital was using a vaporizer to moisturize the air to help Kara breathe. Kara had developed a fever and a cough. Ann and Tommy were taking turns standing by her bed. Now, Dr. Wester had arrived and they all were at her bedside. Ann and Tommy pleaded with Dr. Wester to help.

The Victoris and Shinskis had all arrived earlier, and after seeing and listening to Kara, they began to pray. Ann and Tommy were crying and tears were also coming to Dr. Wester's eyes. The grandparents were at the doorway. The local priest was also present. They were all asking God to help Kara. They all prayed on their knees, looking up to God to help Kara, tears running down their faces.

Just after midnight, on June 10, her birthday, Kara Victori passed out of this world on her way to heaven.

When Dr. Wester told the parents and grandparents that Kara was gone, Mary Victori-O'Neil took over. She knew that God had given her powers to face the world after the death of her husband. She had to use those powers to save Tommy and Ann.

Ann and Tommy were inconsolable, broken hearted. They hugged each other, tearfully. They could not understand how God could be so cruel as to take their daughter, beautiful one-year-old Kara. Kara, whom they loved so profoundly. Kara who had just began to live. Kara who had her whole life before her.

What was the reason for believing in a God who could take your firstborn from you on her first birthday?

Ann and Tommy couldn't sleep. At times they dozed from exhaustion and woke up from nightmares that had them screaming. Mary finally got them to swallow Dr. Wester's sleeping pills. Mary and Mike O'Neil and the Shinskis made arrangements for the funeral, but they could not bury Kara until Ann and Tommy gained a measure of control.

Harry Shinski, the twins, Paul and Jimmy, and Kay were so badly shaken, they had trouble forcing themselves to stop crying to help Ann and Tommy.

A couple of days later, the funeral was held at the Catholic Church in Gilmore and Kara was buried on the lot with Marion at the Holy Name Cemetery in Gilmore.

Tommy and Ann hurried home after the funeral, trying to get some relief by being nearer to Kara by being in her room and holding her toys. Mary and Mike, Steve and Agnes Shinski, Harry, Paul, Jimmy, and Kay stayed at the family luncheon at the Knights of Columbus building just long enough to accept condolences from relatives and friends.

Then Mary said, "Agnes and I are going to Tommy and Ann's house. We know they want to be alone. However, Agnes and I think they need family. Wait for half an hour, and then follow us."

Tommy and Ann were glad to see their mothers. Four people in tears were better than two. Mike, Paul, Jimmy, and Kay came followed by Harry. They brought some food from the Knights of Columbus Hall. They said, "We know you don't want to eat now. We'll put it in the refrigerator for tonight and tomorrow."

Mary said, "When your dad died, I wanted to die. I had my children and you have your families that will be here at all times."

After a short time, the families departed. Tommy and Ann went to bed in each other's arms.

They stayed away from church for a month, even though the Gilmore priest of their youth and their new priest of Carmount called on them repeatedly.

Ann was thankful there was no school, but Tommy reported to the State's Attorney's Office daily.

As the weeks went by, Ann was looking forward to going to school and meeting her new first graders. It turned out that every one of the children, the teachers, her principal, the secretaries, and the janitors made their condolences known to her. She began to feel better, although each night she prayed for Kara and her pillow and Tommy's pillow continued to be wet from their tears.

Now Tommy and Ann had a complete understanding of what Mary meant when she said, "It takes courage. The nights are long."

Forty-five

Almost surprisingly to Tommy and Ann, life went on. Their life fell back into the pre-Kara routine, even though a dozen times a day Kara was in their thoughts.

After school started, Mike and Mary came over one evening to take Tommy and Ann to supper. When they came back to the younger's Victori house, Mary asked to see Kara's room. Ann and Tommy led the way. They hesitated at the door with tears in their eyes. Mary and Mike followed; Mary looked around the room and realized that the room had not changed since Kara's sad death.

Mary said to Ann as she put her arms around her, "You and Tommy will never forget Kara. She will always remain your baby, but I'm sure God will send you other children. No other child will ever take her place. You'll only think of them as Kara's brothers and sisters."

Ann replied, "I'm sure you are right, but it is so difficult."

Tommy put in, "We'll make it, Mother. We'll make it." Then he turned to Mike and said, "We all need a cold drink."

Mike answered, "We have been here before. I'll go to the kitchen and serve all of you."

Forty-six

Jack Wenz, Leo Macy, and Oscar Fell had done all they could to help Tommy and Ann during the sad summer months of Kara's departure. They and their wives were at the wake and funeral. They had driven over several times in two cars, calling the Victoris first, and taking them out to dinner and the last time it was the Illinois State Fair.

This was the last year of school for all four of them. The law school had many mock trials during their senior year. They realized that a trial is a method of settling disputes verbally in a court of law. People on each side of a dispute use lawyers to represent their views, present evidence or question witnesses.

About half of the trials in the United States are jury trials. In the other trials, the defendant chooses to be tried by a judge or a panel of judges instead of a jury. All trials are conducted in a similar manner.

There are two types of trials, civil trials and criminal trials. Civil trials settle non-criminal matters such as contracts, ownership of property, and payment for personal injury. In criminal trials, the jury decides the legal guilt or innocence of a person accused of a crime.

The southern foursome, as the Springfield classmates called Tommy, Jack, Leo, and Oscar, always seemed to come prepared. They had slowed their travel time to one hour. During that time each person assigned a lesson plan would look up the law and that way they put four heads together and discussed the cases. The law evolved and they usually had three or four different opinions, even if one or two had to play devil's advocate.

Jack and Tommy had already decided that they would go half hog. They would keep their teaching jobs for at least one more year, go into partnership together in Gilmore, and serve mainly Gilmore and the mining areas around Gilmore.

Since Ann already taught in Gilmore, she and Tommy had decided that after one more year in Carmount if the law office produced enough revenue, they would sell their house in Carmount and buy one in Gilmore.

It seemed difficult for Mike and Mary to get much time together.

Their work kept them both busy and then there was the coming of Kara, the graduation of Kay from high school, the twins' graduation from the school of engineering at the University of Illinois, then the illness and death of Kara.

As Mary and Michael were in bed when the new school year started, Mary said, "Jimmy and Paul have moved to their new apartment in Springfield and we just came back from taking Kay to Champaign, here we are by ourselves. You know things are so quiet and peaceful. I should be relaxed and happy, but tell me why I'm still apprehensive?"

Mike answered, "So many things have happened since we got married. We have always been on the run. One thinks, surely it just doesn't stop here. What next?"

They both laughed and kissed good night.

The Great Depression started with the market crash of October 29, 1929 when stock holders panicked and sold record shares of stocks. Thousands of people lost huge sums of money as stock values fell. Banks and businesses lost so much that they had to close.

In earlier depressions, business activity had started to pick up after one or two years. But from October 29, 1929 until the end of the Hoover era business slumped. Bank failures increased as the Depression continued. There were 1,350 bank failures in 1930, about 2,300 in 1931, and 1932 started badly.

Human suffering became a reality for millions of Americans. Thousands of families lost their homes. Thousands of farmers lost their farms, and thousands of businesses went under. Many millions and high percentages of people were unemployed.

Illinois and Limbo County had their share of the Great Depression. Banks in Gilmore and Carmount went broke and could not give depositors back their money. Miners lost their homes, and farmers lost their farms.

Wages for those who had a job were low. After a long strike, the United Mineworkers settled for a basic wage of five dollars a day, clerks in stores two dollars a day, teachers in elementary schools between seventy-five and hundred dollars a month for the school year, high school teachers between one thousand and fifteen hundred dollars per year, and farmers twenty-five cents for a bushel of corn or wheat. The average income in the United States was fifteen hundred dollars a year. The Dow Jones average was below one hundred. A loaf of bread was ten cents; a gallon of gas was ten cents; a gallon of milk was forty-five cents; new cars were six hundred dollars; and a new house was under six thousand dollars.

Carmount College was two hundred dollars a year. This included room, board, tuition, and fifteen hours a week of work in the college work program. Illinois College in Jacksonville had two-hundred-dollar a year tuition and the University of Illinois had tuition of one hundred dollars a year.

Mary Victori-O'Neil had a niece working in the Gilmore bank that went under. She warned her aunt to transfer the few hundred dollars she had in the bank to the United States Post Office where the money turned out to be safe and paid two percent interest per year. Otherwise, the Victori children would not have been able to go to college.

The Superior miners were fortunate. They were owned by the North Railroad, but the Hinders Mine was questionable because only part of its coal was sold to the North Railroad and the mine slowed to three days a week. Mary Victori-O'Neil had to be careful of the credit given to miners' families; even Hamburg's and the red light district had noticeable downs.

Mike came home one evening in January 1932 and said to Mary, "I wish I had good news to tell you."

Mary looked up from the evening *St. Louis Post-Dispatch* and said, "If it is bad news, I don't want to hear it."

Mike answered, "Okay, you can read it in next week's *Post*."

Mary changed her mind and said, "Go ahead."

Mike said, "The North Railroad that owns the Superior Mine is planning on bringing in hogs and conveyors, continuous belts that start at the loading places and go all the way to the cages. Slate pickers will pick the slate and the clean coal will be dumped into clean freight coal cars ready to be shipped. The Superior Mines will need less men. The small coal cars would be eliminated, and these continuous belts will save a lot of manpower."

Mary asked, "Do you think that the Hinders Mine will eventually close?"

Michael answered sadly, "Eventually, yes. However, now the good news. The John Sampson Coal Company has signed a contract with the Illinois Power Company, electric utility generator plants, to furnish coal to produce electricity. The mine will work four and five days a week in winter and three to four days in the summer."

Mary said, "Thank goodness."

Mike replied, "The age of machinery has just got a good start. As Tommy could tell you from his study of science, man has just reached the surface. What things will be like fifty to one hundred years from now we can't even imagine."

Forty-seven

Tommy was having a question-answer session in his chemistry class when one of his students put up his hand and said, "Do you mind, Mr. Victori, if I ask you a personal question?"

Tommy said, "No, go ahead."

The student said, "You have been teaching chemistry and physics in Carmount High School for four years. We have enjoyed your classes. We know you are going to law school at night. Are you going to give up your teaching and practice law?"

Tommy smiled and said, "That is a question I've been asking myself. I think teaching is a wonderful vocation and I really enjoy teaching chemistry and physics. We all have choices to make. Do we want to go to college? If so, what field, or vocational school? Or what about going to a job right out of high school? Most of us will have more than one job and often in different fields. Right now I plan on returning to Carmount High School next year and be a part-time lawyer. I hope to keep both options open until I make a final decision."

The students responded by giving a round of applause.

Tommy said, "Thank you."

When Tommy and Jack were going to Litchfield that evening. Tommy told Jack about the student's question, even though he knew he would have to repeat it for his Litchfield classmates.

Jack Wenz said, "What about me? I'm an elementary teacher at Gilmore. I think our going together in one law office will cut our expenses, secretary, rent, utilities, supplies, etc, almost in half. Which will be necessary because even when we get clients, cases last for months and even years. You are right; we'll have to teach another year or two."

When they told Leo May and Oscar Fell about the question and their plans. May said, "I'm a teacher too and our salaries are low. I'll have to have an income while I'm setting up a law office."

Oscar Fell said, "At least you guys have jobs and some income. Banks all over the United States, Illinois and Montgomery County are going broke. I'm holding my breath that next week I may be unemployed. We, in the banking business, are looking forward to Congress passing a banking act which will establish a Federal Deposit Insurance Corporation which will insure the people's money so they won't be afraid of depositing it in our banks. So far, all we have had is talk. I don't think the Hoover Administration will get it done. It will take a new president and a new Congress to get it done. I have been a Republican, but I can easily change if it is my bread and butter."

Tommy said, "When I went to work at Ed Feld's office, an elected Democratic State's Attorney, I had to make a decision. It was easy. I joined the Young Democrats Club in Limbo County."

Jack said, "I joined the Young Democrats of Limbo County several years ago. We all have our reasons. I had mine."

Leo May said, "As a teacher, I wanted to stay neutral in politics, and up to now, I'm not active in either party. I realize when I become a lawyer I'll probably make a decision."

Oscar Fell said, "The national presidential nominating conventions are coming up this summer with the elections this fall. I'm hoping the Republicans don't renominate Hoover because, the way things are in the United States, he doesn't stand a chance."

Leo May said, "Oscar, I think you are right, but the way party conventions are set up, it is very difficult to dump a sitting president after only one term."

Forty-eight

The twins, Jimmy and Paul, were living in their apartment in Springfield. They were working for the Department of Transportation for the State of Illinois. They had accepted the Depression salaries of one hundred twenty-five dollars a month and realized that there were many engineers graduating in 1931, from universities all over the United States, who were unemployed.

Paul and Jimmy were so impressed with first Tommy's 1924 Dodge, then his 1930 Dodge that they bought a 1930 Dodge that looked like new and had less than five thousand miles for three hundred dollars. They drove to work at the Illinois Department of Transportation in their 1930 Dodge. Usually, they worked at the department headquarters. However, if one of them went out on a job, he would use a state vehicle.

They had met several young ladies at church functions, but as yet were unattached. Paul and Jimmy had even ventured out in the Springfield red light district which made those in Limbo County look small by comparison. After a couple of such trips, the two small-town coal miners' sons decided to stay close to the church functions.

Kay did not feel lost at the University of Illinois because she had been there several times with the twins, and her boyfriend, Harry Barnes, now a sophomore, had invited her to several dances the preceding year. However, there was only one word that described the size of the University of Illinois and the number of students, and that was big as in BIG.

Kay had decided that she was going to be a business education teacher, majoring in typing, shorthand, and bookkeeping, keeping in mind that if she didn't like teaching she could transfer to the business world.

She knew that she would not see Harry during the school day, but there were many places where students who were interested in each other could meet, including the library on campus and the theater off campus.

Tommy and Ann decided that they would let nature take its course. There would be no condoms or other prophylactics to guard against the birth of a second child. In their hearts they wanted another child, preferably a girl, but even a boy would be welcome.

Ann had her elementary teaching job to keep her busy and many little girls and boys to hug, as well as the housework and cooking. As busy as Ann was, Tommy seemed to always be on the go with his chemistry and physics classes, both of which required laboratory preparation, the three trips each week to Lincoln Law School in Springfield, law study and a couple hours travel time each school session.

When Tommy came home at midnight each Friday night, he would embrace Ann with, "Thank God for weekends."

Mary and Mike O'Neil seemed to be the only ones in the family that had settled down to a relaxing life. They were alone most of the time in the Victori-O'Neil building, except when the children came home, which at first was every two weeks and now was closer to every two months.

Mary still took care of the store, but she had shortened the store hours so that she only worked seven hours a day during the week, eight on Saturday, and was closed all day on Sunday. Mike had regular eight-hour days at the mine, Monday through Friday. Although, as a boss, he was subject to calls at all hours.

All Americans looked forward to the National Convention in 1932. The Republicans re-nominated Herbert Hoover for president and Charles Curtis for vice-president. The Democrats nominated Governor Franklin D. Roosevelt of New York for president and Speaker of the House John H. Garner of Texas for vice-president.

Hoover was reluctant to interfere with the American economy. He called the Depression "a temporary halt in the prosperity of a great people." At first he depended on business companies and industries to solve their own problems, then he requested Congress to pass laws enabling the government to help businesses. One of these laws set up the Reconstruction Finance Corporation which loaned money to banks to keep them from going bankrupt. Hoover believed that the states and local communities should provide relief for jobless workers, even when it became clear that the unemployed needed much more help.

Hoover supported many public works and conservation programs, but they continually needed more and more. Things got so bad that by the election of 1932, the Republicans had little hope of winning.

Roosevelt promised a "New Deal." He promised to provide relief for the unemployed, to help farmers, and to end prohibition. The easiest promise to keep was to end prohibition, even though it took a new amendment to the Constitution. In 1933, prohibition ended.

Congress, under Roosevelt, passed many laws to try to help the new president keep his promises. At his request, Congress passed the Federal Emergency Relief Administration Act and appropriated five hundred million dollars to help states and cities. These funds put people to work building streets, bridges, roads, schools, post offices, and other public buildings. He established the Civilian Conservation Corps for young people to do public work and the Works Progress Administration to provide work for people without jobs. The money was raised partly by raising taxes and partly by borrowing. The economy did improve but slowly as debt increased.

Tommy Victori, Jack Wenz, Leo May, and Oscar Fell all graduated from Lincoln Law School in the spring of 1932. The long four-year period of working full-time jobs in the daytime and making a round trip of nearly one hundred miles three nights a week was over. Now what? Decisions, decisions, decisions.

One decision was easy. Since they went to school for four years together, they would celebrate together. They chose the Gardens in Litchfield, and they had a private section set aside that Saturday night for the graduation festival. They, their wives, and their families had an informal luncheon, including sodas and beverages. Everyone had a good time, including Ann who was expecting another baby in August.

When Tommy and Ann reached home in Carmount, Ann was exhausted. It was only ten o'clock, as Tommy and Ann had left the celebration early. Ann hurried into the bedroom to lie down. Tommy followed solicitously to see if there was anything he could do to help.

Ann's mother, Agnes, and Tommy's mother, Mary, were on the phone or coming over more often as Ann's pregnancy seemed to worry both of them. They even cheated a little by letting each other know they made calls so they could get twice as much information by calling half as often.

As June progressed, Ann and Tommy began to worry more, telling each other that there was no need to worry. They thought of changing doctors. Ed Webster had delivered Kara into the world and had been present when she died of pneumonia. Then they recalled how they saw Dr. Wester in tears when he told them that Kara was gone. That did it. There was no more discussion about changing doctors.

Tommy and Jack were fortunate enough to rent a four-room downstairs office. They had a waiting room, an office for each of them, and a library room. They advertised in the Gilmore paper and put up a sign in the window, Jack Wenz and Tommy Victori, Attorneys at Law. They hired a woman who had worked for a local retired attorney as their secretary, which was a fortunate hiring as they had an experienced secretary.

The announcement in the *Gilmore News* stated that they would be in their office at nine A.M. the first Monday in June 1932. Their first clients were relatives who wanted wills made. Tommy and Jack used the Limbo County legal directory for suggested fees.

Their first big case was the Gilmore superintendent of schools, who represented the local Board of Education and wanted to hire them on a contingency basis for a fee of two hundred dollars a year plus an hourly fee for any work done.

The superintendent met with both men and introduced himself as Earl J. Smith. He had been superintendent of the Gilmore schools for the last two years and had a list of cases and the various functions performed by Fred Blossom, their predecessor who had retired. After looking over the work done by Fred Blossom they realized that handling elections for the school district, bond issues, and above all, going to court nearly every year to try to get the assessed valuations of the North Railroad and Superior Mines raised would be their most important duties.

Jack and Tommy took a day to go to the Carmount County Courthouse to study the district court files for the last ten years against the North Railroad and the Superior Mines. They were long and drawn out. They always started out in the Limbo County Circuit Court and went to the State Appellate Court and a couple times to the State Supreme Court. The payoff was that the Gilmore school district had been rewarded by having the assessed valuations raised repeatedly, which meant that the district collected thousands of dollars more in taxes. When the assessed valuation was raised, it usually stayed at the higher level.

It was midnight on July 29, when Ann started having pains. They called Dr. Wester when the pains were a half an hour apart. He said to Tommy, "Tell Ann to get ready to go to the hospital."

Before they went to the hospital, which was only a few blocks away, Ann called her mother, Agnes, and told her to call Tommy's mother, Mary.

Ann was taken to the delivery room, Agnes and Mary arrived. They were allowed to see Ann for a few minutes.

As Ann was taken to the delivery room, Tommy, Mrs. Shinski, and Mrs. O'Neil went to the waiting room. They all recalled when Kara was born and how happy they were. However, they could never forget how short her life was on earth.

About two hours later, Dr. Wester came out and said, "Congratulations to Tommy. You have a healthy baby boy."

Tommy shook Dr. Wester's hand and said, "Thank you. When can I go see them?"

Dr. Wester said, "Give the nurses another thirty minutes to get the mother and baby ready."

The two grandmothers and Tommy hugged each other.

When one of the nurses came to the waiting room, Tommy and the grandmothers hurried to Ann's room. Ann was sitting up with Marion Thomas Victori in her arms, with tears of joy in her eyes. Tommy hugged them. The grandmothers then took their turns, Agnes Shinski, and then Mary Victori-O'Neil.

The grandmothers headed back to Hinders to spread the good news and try to get a little sleep, as it was five o'clock in the morning. Tommy hurried to his home a few blocks away to get a little shut-eye.

That day Harry Shinski, the twins, Paul and Jimmy, and Kay had to see the new baby and congratulate the mother and father. The grandfather, Steve Shinski, and step-grandfather, Mike O'Neil, had their turns visiting Ann and Marion Thomas Victori.

When Ann and Marion came home from the hospital, history seemed to be repeating itself to them. Ann decided to nurse the baby for the first two weeks, and then change him over to the bottle before going back to teaching. Every time Marion awakened and started crying, Ann and Tommy felt like they were going to attend to Kara again.

The feeling made them feel good and bad at the same time. They even discussed it with each other. They began to wonder if they should consult a psychologist or a psychiatrist. They decided to tough it out, realizing that only people who had gone through the same experience with their first child could understand this feeling about the second baby.

As the nights went by, Ann and Tommy continued talking to each other about the similarities and the differences. After a couple of months, it all blended into one as they realized that Marion was a brother, but not Kara.

Life went on, Tommy and Jack took care of the law business in July and August and received enough money to pay the rent, utilities, the secretary's salary, and other expenses with a balance of a couple hundred dollars in the bank. The big question was now with school starting, and Jack going to the Gilmore Elementary School to teach and Tommy reporting to the Carmount High School, what kind of office hours would they have?

They decided they would have office hours together from seven to nine in the evening on Tuesdays and Thursdays and nine to noon on Saturday mornings. They would use Monday, Wednesday, and Friday evenings for special appointments.

As soon as Tommy and Jack saw in the paper that the Superior Mine was going to hogs, and conveyor belts, they investigated the cost of going from hand loading to mechanization. The North Railroad, which owned the four large Superior Coal Mines, would have to spend millions of dollars. This meant that the assessed valuation of the mines would go up accordingly. Tommy and Jack met with the Board of Education and school superintendent and agreed to try to work out a compromise that would be fair to the company and the school district without going to court.

As the school year went by, Jack and Tommy decided to hand in their resignations early so that the school districts would have plenty of time to find replacements.

They realized that if they wanted to make a living as lawyers they would both have to work full-time in their profession.

Forty-nine

After Tommy turned in his resignation to Carmount High School, he realized that this would probably be his last year teaching chemistry and physics. First his students, then his subjects became more important to him. He had always liked teaching, and now his career was ending after only five years.

He went home and discussed his concerns with Ann as she was giving Marion his bottle before putting him to sleep. As soon as the baby was asleep and Ann put him in his bed, she turned her attention to Tommy.

Ann said, "You know, Tommy, I have been teaching two years longer than you, and I have just finished my degree, piecemeal, in seven years after getting my certificate. I've been looking forward to the day when my lawyer husband would be making so much money that I could retire. Now, I don't know that I want to quit teaching, regardless of how much money my husband makes. I like teaching. My first graders are always so eager to learn that they inspire me to look forward to tomorrow. They were especially helpful after Kara left us. No, don't count on me giving up teaching."

Tommy answered, "I can understand that. I feel that way right now, but I have no choice, I must give my legal profession a chance.

"As you know, Jack Wenz is my law partner. He has turned in his resignation to Gilmore Elementary School, your school system. In our cases there would have been no need of four years of night law school if we had decided

147

to stay in teaching. He and I have talked and we are both glad that we put in the time, effort, and money. Time will tell if we made the right decision."

Tommy and Jack had a couple of divorce cases. They had discussed how they would handle divorce cases. The most difficult ones were when there were children involved; the division of assets, who would get the house, what about child support, etc.

As Tommy listened to other people's problems he realized how lucky he and Ann were. The saddest part when children were involved was who would get the children and visitation rights. Usually the mother got the children and the house. There were always complications like a third person, a man or woman waiting for a divorce and a marriage. Generally, he had a lawyer and she had a lawyer and not enough money to pay expenses. After a couple of experiences, Tommy and Jack decided that they would avoid divorce cases when possible.

Tommy and Jack were active young Democrats. Jack was elected vice-president of the Limbo County Young Democrats. They were active in the Governor Henry Horner's campaign and Franklin D. Roosevelt's campaign. It was the Great Depression, and the county, state, and nation went democratic.

As long as they were teaching, Tommy and Jack were not interested in a full time or part time job in politics. This would change, however, with the end of the school year. Until they had enough business to necessitate their working full time in their law practice, a job in politics would help their income.

Tommy, who had worked part time in the State's Attorney's Office during summers when he was in law school, was interested in one day running for State's Attorney. Therefore, he wanted to become an Assistant State's Attorney. Jack Wenz was looking for a state job and wanted to work part-time for the Attorney General in Limbo County.

Since the Democrats were elected in the county, state, and nation, they looked forward to summer and fall and getting part-time jobs.

Tommy was going to go to the weekend income tax schools, and Jack was going to handle most estates. General law in small counties involved many fields, and they wanted to handle all they could.

It was getting more and more difficult for the Victori-O'Neil children to get together. However, they still managed to get to dinners for holidays, particularly Thanksgiving, Christmas and Easter.

The O'Neils, the Shinskis, the twins, Paul and Jimmy, and Kay all seemed able to call on Tommy and Ann and Marion. They all wanted to see the baby. They brought him toys and clothing until Ann finally thanked them and said that it would be much better to start a savings program for the future.

When the school year ended, Tommy and Ann decided that they should take a vacation. They packed a couple of suitcases and baby Marion's stroller, buggy, play pen, bottles, and supplies and headed for the Ozarks in their latest Dodge, a 1930 Model.

They were going to Bagnell Dam and Osage Beach. They had not made reservations, but had been told by friends that had been there that they would have no trouble getting a room. They tried three places that looked satisfactory before they decided on Oak Inn, which had a swimming pool. They also wanted to be near the Dam where the shopping and entertainment places were and wanted to spend an evening at the Ozark Opry.

Bagnell Dam was over two hundred miles from Carmount, so they started from home Tuesday morning on a beautiful June day and arrived at their destination in the middle of the day after eating lunch on the way.

They checked in at the Oak Inn and then decided to put Marion down for a nap while they unpacked and laid down for a little shut-eye, too. A couple of hours later, they put the buggy in the car and drove to the Bagnell Dam area. Tommy pushed the buggy with Marion riding joyfully while they looked at various displays for sale. Homemade wooden trinkets, wooden buckets, and ornaments of all kinds were on display. There were all kinds of things to eat; cookies, cakes, candies, ice cream, and sandwiches, including hamburgers and hot dogs.

Tommy and Ann drove over to the Ozark Opry and bought tickets for the eight o'clock show that evening. They had noticed a nice restaurant called The Class, near their motel. They went back to the motel to change and feed Marion, and then they went out to eat. After supper, they went back to the motel, which had a babysitting service, but they decided to take Marion with them to the Ozark Opry and take turns holding him during the two-hour show.

They parked at the Ozark Opry parking lot and located a place that rented baby carrying baskets. They rented a basket and Tommy carried Marion into the Ozark Opry Show building.

The singing and the music were enjoyable. The jokes were a little corny at times but funny. The dress and costumes were Ozark. Marion slept most of the time and Ann and Tommy were really able to relax and feel as though they didn't have a care in the world.

As Tommy picked up the basket with Marion, he and Ann saw a couple approaching them. Tommy thought, *I know him. He's Jerry Beys, the fellow who graduated with me and Ann from high school in Gilmore in 1924, nine years ago.*

As Tommy and Jerry shook hands, Jerry introduced his wife to Ann and Tommy. Tommy said, "I'm happy to meet you too, Susan Beys."

Ann also shook hands with Jerry and expressed her pleasure at the introduction.

Tommy said, "The Gilmore High School Class of 1924, where have you been these last nine years?"

Jerry said, "I went to business school in St. Louis, Missouri. We now live in Springfield, Missouri."

Tommy said, "We both teach in Limbo County. Ann in Gilmore; and I in Carmount. How long are you here? Maybe we can get together for lunch tomorrow."

Jerry said, "That sounds good. Do you have any questions?"

Tommy said, "We are staying at the Oak Inn. We just ate at The Class."

Jerry said, "We know where it is. We'll meet you there at twelve noon tomorrow."

Susan said, "Tell us about your baby."

Ann said, "He is a boy. His name is Marion."

Tommy said, "We are looking forward to lunch tomorrow."

Jerry answered, "So are we."

With a wave, they parted. Tommy said to Ann, "What a pleasant surprise."

Ann answered, "When you run into a classmate nine years later in the Ozarks, wow!"

The next day was a beautiful day in June. Since they were meeting the Beys for lunch at The Class, they decided they would wait until the heat of the afternoon to go swimming.

When they arrived for lunch, pushing Marion in the buggy, the Beys were already waiting for them. The Beys bent over the buggy so they could get a better look at Marion.

Ann had fed Marion before they came so he was half asleep. Susan said, "After we eat, if he is awake, can I hold him?"

Ann said, "You sure can."

They all ordered a light lunch and coffee. Then, after lunch, while Susan was holding Marion, Ann and Tommy told Jerry and Susan Beys the sad story of their first born, Kara Victori. Jerry and Susan sat there, almost unbelieving. Finally, Jerry said, "On her first birthday?"

And Susan echoed, "It doesn't seem possible."

Jerry called for another round of coffee. Then he said, "We have been married three years. There have been no children. Yes, we want children," and with a laugh, he added, "We'll keep trying."

Changing the subject, Tommy said, "When I said I was teaching at the Carmount High School that was correct for the last five years. The first four years I went to Lincoln Law School in Springfield at night. Now, I have resigned the Carmount teaching job to practice law full time."

Jerry said, "As I told you, I went to business school, and now I manage a Sears store in Springfield. My wife, Susan, is a nurse at the local hospital."

Tommy said, "This is Wednesday, we leave Friday. I promised my partner, Jack Wenz, I would take care of business on Saturday."

Jerry said, "We leave tomorrow morning. We'll exchange addresses and phone numbers. When we get to Limbo County, we'll look you up."

Tommy got up and shook hands with Jerry and waited for Susan to hand Marion to Ann and then shook hands with her. Then he said, "Be sure to look us up when you come to Limbo."

Susan and Jerry and Ann all nodded.

Fifty

Friday, on the way home, the Victoris stopped by the O'Neils. It was late afternoon and both Mike and Mary were in the store. Mary, after greeting them and taking Marion in her arms said, "You are just in time for supper."

Tommy said, "I don't know, Mom. We've been gone from home for four days."

Ann said, "You didn't know we were coming."

Mary and Mike both replied, "You have to eat supper somewhere. It might just as well be here."

Mary added, "Jimmy, Paul and Kay are all going to be here for supper. It will be nice having the whole family."

In the end, Tommy, Ann, and Marion all waited for Mary to go into the kitchen. Ann went with her while Tommy and Mike took care of Marion.

Kay was the first one to arrive. She still worked in the store in summer and had been shopping. She was happy to see Tommy, Ann and Marion. She asked, "Are you home from your Ozark vacation so soon?"

Tommy answered, "Yes, I promised Jack Wenz that I would take care of the law office tomorrow."

Mike asked, "How was your vacation?"

Tommy said, "It was fun and relaxing. You are right. It is too bad that we couldn't stay a few more days."

As they were sitting down for supper, the twins came in a rush, said hello, and went to the bathroom to wash. Tommy put Marion in the family high chair and they all sat down while Michael O'Neil gave the prayer. "We thank you, Lord for this pleasant family gathering. Bless us and bless this food to our bodies. Amen."

The twins were the first to speak. Paul asked, "How were the Ozarks?"

Jimmy said, "I was going to ask the same question."

Ann answered, "We had a good time, but the vacation was too short. Even Marion enjoyed the water in the swimming pool. You know I think this new idea of teaching babies to swim will catch on if all babies take to the water like Marion."

Tommy added, "You should have seen him splashing like a duck to water."

Ann added, "Now it is your turn, Kay, and the twins."

Kay answered, "My English and required courses are okay, but I'll be glad when I get more into my business major."

Jimmy spoke up first, "We are both working on a new bridge to cross the Illinois River at Meredosia. It is going to be high in the sky."

Paul added, "Jimmy said it all."

Mary said, "This is nice. Don't you think so, Mike? We should invite all of you to supper more often."

Mike said, "You are right, Mary. We are getting more information than we normally receive in months."

Tommy and Ann stayed longer than they intended. Ann finally picked up Marion and said to Tommy, "Let's go." After bidding farewell to all the others, the Victoris left.

Mary asked the twins, "Why don't you stay overnight?"

Jimmy looked at Paul, "Tell Mom we brought clothes for the weekend. We'll join Kay and all go to Hamburg's. It's a chance to see if we know anybody there anymore."

Kay spoke up, "You'll know most of the people there. They are just a little older."

Mike laughed, "Your mom and I join in very often."

Kay chimed in, "You know I still go with Harry Barnes. What about you guys? Any new girlfriends?"

Paul put in, "We like single life so well that we'll probably stay bachelors."

Fifty-one

Tommy reported to the law office before nine in the morning on Saturday. Jack Wenz was already there. Tommy said, "I thought you would be gone this weekend."

Jack answered, "I am just here long enough to tell you about an accident case we have involving two sisters. The sister who was driving received minor injuries; the passenger sister was badly injured. We have no choice but to sue the driver and her insurance company."

Jack had the case written up and explained it to Tommy. "The sister that was the passenger cautioned the driver sister a couple of times to slow down, but the driver laughed at the passenger. The driver took a turn too fast and turned the car over and the passenger sister was badly injured.

"The sisters' names were Alberta, the driver, and Roberta. They were twins, unmarried, and close to each other. The father will be in at ten o'clock. I took the case on a contingency."

Mr. Ralph Brown, the father of the twins, came in and was introduced to Tommy Victori. Tommy, after shaking hands with Mr. Brown, asked, "How is Roberta?"

Mr. Brown, tears coming to his eyes, said, "She is going to make it, but she is going to lose her left hand."

Tommy expressed his sorrow and said, to Mr. Brown, "The insurance policy has a fifty-thousand-dollar limitation. We should get the company to pay the maximum."

Jack Wenz said, "I agree."

157

Ralph Brown stayed in a few minutes, and then departed. Jack Wenz then left and Tommy was left alone, as the secretary did not work on Saturday.

Tommy looked through the current cases folder and realized that business was picking up, but they would need a good deal more clients to be successful.

Before lunch, he decided to go to the country road near Bunker Hill and look at the turn where the Brown accident took place. The curve on the country road where the accident happened was nearly a square turn. He drove the road again to check the warning signs. There was a warning sign that read SHARP TURN AHEAD and a sign for the turn. Evidently, Alberta had been careless. Although she claimed that she was going less than thirty miles per hour when she hit the turn.

Tommy went back to his office in Gilmore. He made a few notes, shook his head, got back in his Dodge, and headed for home.

On Sunday, Tommy told Ann, "I'd like to take you to Meredosia and see the bridge on the Illinois River that Paul and Jimmy are building, and stop at the Meredosia Café and eat some good Illinois River catfish."

Ann said, "That sounds good to me, but I don't think Marion is old enough for catfish."

Tommy said, "He'll settle for his bottle, but he is hungry for baby food."

They left Carmount about ten o'clock in the morning and reached Meredosia before noon. The Illinois River Bridge was taking shape, and as Jimmy and Paul had told them, it seemed to be reaching for the sky.

Tommy said, "You know we must compliment the twins. This going to be a magnificent bridge."

Ann replied, "You are right. We are proud of our teaching, but I must admit that the civil engineers that plan our roads and bridges contribute a good deal to our communities, state, and nation."

They stopped in the Meredosia Café parking lot, picked up Marion, and went inside. They were met at the door, and a waitress brought over a highchair and led them to a table. Tommy and Ann both ordered fried catfish, a baked potato, green beans, and a Coke. Marion seemed content with his bottle.

It was a beautiful June day and life seemed to be smiling at Ann and Tommy again.

Fifty-two

Tommy and Jack were both in the office one day when a young lady who appeared to be pregnant, wearing maternity clothes, was shown to Tommy's office. Tommy stood up as his secretary brought the young lady to his office and introduced her as Miss Betty Sanders.

Miss Sanders sat down and said, "I live in Kollinson and my family is a friend of your Aunt Ann Favero and her family. I have a problem, and since I am a school teacher, your aunt said I should go to see two retired school teachers who are now full-time lawyers."

Tommy was looking askance at Betty Sanders, and then asked, "How can I help?"

Betty asked, "Is your partner in?"

Tommy answered, "Jack Wenz is in his office."

Betty said, "Can you get him? I want to tell my story to both of you at once."

Tommy said, "I sure can." Then he went to Jack's office, brought him back, and introduced him to Betty Sanders.

They all sat down and Betty said, "I teach in a town adjoining Kollinson." She hesitated and then went on, "As my appearance indicates, I'm pregnant and not married. The father of the baby will get his divorce next week. We plan to marry that weekend. The Board of Education of the district has already fired me for immorality. The legal question is, can they do that? I'd like to have my job back."

Tommy spoke first, "We would have to do some research on the question."

Jack added, "We have to determine whether the Board of Education acted legally."

Betty said, "Will you take my case?"

Tommy said, "We will be glad to take your case if we think we can help you."

Betty Sanders said, "This did not happen during the school hours and certainly not on school property. The pregnancy is not related to my job. The baby will be born in August. I could have easily finished the school year."

Jack spoke, "Tommy and I will talk this over. If you will wait in the waiting room, we'll let you know whether we will take your case."

Betty Sander said, "I'll wait, because I want your help."

Jack turned to Tommy and said, "This case is a challenge, and we need the court experience."

Tommy answered, "I agree with you, but let's look up the Illinois School Law on teacher dismissal and find out if she has a contract with tenure, and if she belongs to the teacher's union or the Illinois Education Association."

Twenty minutes later, Tommy went to the waiting room and asked Miss Sanders to come into his office. He said, "Please sit down, Miss Sanders. We have decided we will take your case, but we have a few questions we want to ask."

Jack took over. "Do you belong to a teacher's organization?"

Miss Sanders said, "I belong to the I.E.A."

Jack said, "We are familiar with the Illinois Education Association. We both belonged to the I.E.A. before we retired as teachers."

Tommy said, "Do you have a copy of your dismissal notice with you?"

161

Betty Sanders opened her purse and handed the notice to Tommy. Tommy read the dismissal for immorality, effective immediately.

"Have you talked to other lawyers?" asked Jack.

"Only one other firm," answered Betty. "To be honest with you, I did not intend to contest it when I received the dismissal notice in April. I changed my mind, and that is why I'm here now."

Tommy looked at Jack who was nodding his head yes. Jack said, "We talked it over and we'll only require one hundred dollars as a retainer, and we'll take the case. How long have you been teaching in the district?"

Betty Sanders answered, "Five years and have had no problems and have always had good recommendations from my principal and superintendent."

Betty Sanders wrote out a check for one hundred dollars and prepared to leave.

Tommy said, "I'm glad to have met you."

Jack added, "I'll say amen to that, and you can count on us to do our best."

Tommy said, "Now, I'll say amen to my partner's words and add, please come back and see us in a week. We should have more information for you."

After Betty Sanders left, Jack and Tommy sat around and talked. Tommy said, "Jack, we have to know more facts. Judging from the way Betty looks now, at eight months, she certainly didn't show much in March or April. What happened? Did somebody tell the administration? Did the principal call her in and confront her?"

Jack said, "She had a contract. Did they ask her to resign? Did she refuse? She said she was fired."

Tommy said, "She'll be in next week, and we'll find out."

Jack said, "Immorality, not conforming with accepted principles of right and wrong in sexual behavior in this case. Did they follow legal procedures? Only the Board of Education can fire her. Did the Board of Education give her a hearing? Did she have her lawyer present?"

Fifty-three

In the middle of July, Tommy came home one evening and found Ann crying. He immediately went over to her, put his arms around her and asked, "Ann, what is the matter? Why are you crying?"

Ann said, "Marion's first birthday will be in a couple of weeks. We have talked about a first birthday party. I'm worried."

Tommy tried to console her. "Yes, I know you are thinking of what happened to Kara. We can never forget that and we don't want to, but this is our son, Marion Thomas. He is alive and well. Yes, go ahead and invite your family, and I'll invite mine. I think we should invite a few of our close friends. This is an extra special occasion.

"As you know, we had him baptized the first week he was born. Now we are going to celebrate his first birthday."

Ann threw her arms around Tommy and said, "You are a wonderful husband and father. I love you."

Tommy answered, "Thank you, Ann. I love you, too."

The next two weeks went by quickly as they prepared for Marion Thomas' first birthday on July 30, 1933. That evening, the Shinskis were the first to arrive, followed by Mary, Mike, and Kay, then the twins, Paul and Jimmy, followed by Mary's sister, Ann, and her husband and three children. Louis Looke, Dean Basse, and Tony Prima came in followed by Sally Sponick and Mary Bruno.

164

Tommy and Ann knew they would have a crowd so they had decorated the basement with balloons and white, red, and blue crepe paper and put out tables and chairs.

Mary Victori-O'Neil and her husband, Mike, and Harry and the Shinski grandparents brought the food and Tommy and Ann had tubs of ice for the soda and beer.

When everyone was in the basement, Ann brought the guest of honor, Marion Thomas Victori, to the basement. Mary carried the cake she had made with one candle on it to the basement and Agnes Shinski led the group in singing softly, "Happy Birthday to You."

Until the cameras started flashing, no one noticed the photographer. Marion was the center of attention. His proud parents and grandparents, relatives and friends all had their pictures taken.

Marion smiled and laughed enough to please everyone. After Ann put Marion to bed, the entire group ate, drank, and visited until ten o'clock. When everyone had departed, Tommy and Ann went to Marion's bed and hugged each other happily.

Fifty-four

In September, Tommy began to work two days a week in the State's Attorney's Office. Jack worked two days a week in the Limbo County Assistant Attorney General's office. They were careful to have their days arranged to be sure that at least one of them would be in the Gilmore office every day.

Jack and Tommy met with the insurance company that represented the twin sisters. At the first meeting, the insurance representative offered half a loaf. Both Jack and Tommy said no. At the second meeting a week later, Tommy and Jack said they would go to court and ask for a trial by jury.

They had discussed a settlement with their clients and had advised them not to go to court if they could get a settlement of forty thousand dollars plus. Their clients agreed. After a second and third meeting, they all agreed on a forty-five-thousand-dollar figure.

In the meantime, Betty Sanders came back to their office, and told them she had been fired without a hearing, and the Board of Education stopped paying her immediately.

Tommy and Jack went to the Circuit Court in Edwardsville and sued the principal, superintendent, and Alltinon Board of Education for firing Betty Sanders illegally and asked for full payment of her contract, reinstatement in her teaching position, and legal fees. The lawyer for the Board of Education and Administrators met with Tommy and Jack and tried to reach a settlement by paying off her contract.

166

Tommy and Jack said, "No."

They spent two days in court, and Tommy and Jack were able to get the jury to agree to their position. When the verdict came in, Betty Sanders was so happy she continually hugged her lawyers for getting her contract paid, reinstatement in her job, and getting her legal fees paid.

Tommy and Jack were waiting for the right opportunity to go to court protesting the new assessed valuation given the Superior Coal Company mines. Their investigation showed that the North Railroad had spent four million dollars on the equipment, hogs, conveyors, and belts for the four mines. When they found that the new assessment had only increased by five hundred thousand dollars, they went to the Circuit Court in Carmount with the information and sued to have the assessment increased to two million.

The lawyers for the North Railroad argued that it took most of the year to install the equipment and any increase beyond five hundred thousand dollars should be next year. The judge asked for a hearing in his quarters and told them, "Get this settled between you for the next two years at a minimum." Then he left the room.

It took two hours of discussion and debates but they finally agreed to one million for the first year and two million for the second year. Tommy and Jack told them that they had to take this to the Gilmore Board of Education.

The attorneys for the North Railroad and the Superior Coal Company said, "We are ready for a court hearing."

At the next Board of Education meeting, the president of the Board of Education said, "We have been settling in court for less than half a loaf in the ten years I

167

have been on the Gilmore Board. I want to congratulate our lawyers, and I recommend we accept the settlement." The Board of Education accepted the Charles Sims recommendation unanimously.

Tommy and Jack had anticipated that action, and Ann had a babysitter ready. Tommy and Ann met the Wenz couple at the Glades for an evening of celebration as they sang to themselves, "We are in the money now."

Fifty-five

Tommy announced early in 1933 that he would file in December for the State's Attorney's Office since Ed Fels was retiring. There were three filing for the office in the Democrat party, one from the north, one from the center, and Tommy from the south of Limbo County. The Republican Party had no contest since only one filed from the south end of Limbo County.

Tommy organized early. He called a meeting in his office. He started with only a small number of helpers. Attending were Jack Wenz, Mike O'Neil, Harry Shinski, Tony Prima, Dean Basse, Louis Looke, and John Ford, a down to earth democrat who was an economics professor at Carmount College, and Tommy's two brothers, Paul and Jimmy.

Tommy thanked them all for coming and introduced everyone present. "Now, I'm going to turn the meeting over to John Ford. He helped Ed Fels win two terms so I'm happy to have him advise us on procedure."

John said, "I'm happy to help. As all of you know, this is a three-man race. I won't mention names. There is a candidate from the north, one from the center, and Tommy is from the southern end of Limbo County. We'll concentrate on the south, but we have to get some help from the north and center. If you know anyone from the north and center, ask for their help. I have a few people that I intend to ask for help."

Mike O'Neil spoke up. "I'll work on the United Coal Mine Workers for all of Limbo County, and I also have some Irish friends I'll get to help."

spoke up, "We are coal miners, and
ɪe votes."

ɛ up, "We have just started, but we
ɪss people, professional people, union
ɪt forget Democrat Precinct Commit-

ɪd, "I'm a Democratic Precinct Com-
mittee man from Hinders. I go to the county meetings
and know a lot of the fifty-two committee men in the
country. I'll work on them."

John Ford added, "We need all the help we can get.
However, let's not forget that all important thing called
money."

Tommy said, "I'll accept money from legal taverns
and eateries that sell liquor, but I'll not accept money
from taverns that have gambling or houses of prostitution."

After further discussion, John Ford said, "We'll meet
here two weeks from this evening, on November the first.

"Remember, Tommy files in December of 1933 for
the primary, which is in March of 1934, with the election
in November of 1934. They call it an off-year election
because there is no presidential election."

Tommy went home and told Ann about the meeting,
"I started early, but I have to spend a lot of money to
advertise, so my name can become known in Limbo
County. Limbo County has a population of about fifty
thousand. Since this is an off-year election, there will be
not be as many voters, but I expect over ten thousand
votes in the Democratic Primary.

"Ann, you and I will be going to many meetings between now and the Democratic Primary in March of 1934
and many more before the general election in November
of 1934."

Ann said, "Tommy, I know you want to be the State's Attorney of Limbo County, so I'll do everything I can to help you get elected. To me, prosecuting criminals from thieves to murderers seems difficult, but since you worked in the office when you were in law school and now you are Assistant State's Attorney to Ed Fels, you should know what you are getting into." Then Ann shook her head and walked away.

Marion, now over two years old, came running into the house with a sucker that Grandma O'Neil had given him. Tommy picked him up and said, "Mom, please do not give him too much candy."

Ann said nothing, and Mary answered, "That sucker is the only candy I gave him."

Tommy and Ann were now living in Gilmore. They sold their house in Carmount, and bought a six-room house with full basement and double garage for less money than they got for their home in Carmount. Houses were less expensive in Gilmore than the county seat. Tommy and Ann saw a good deal more of the Shinskis and O'Neils now that they were less than three miles from Hinders and of course, there was little need to hire a babysitter.

Tommy went to Carmount two days a week to work in Ed Fels' office; otherwise, he spent most of his time in Gilmore. This made it more convenient for Ann, who was still teaching in Gilmore.

Business was picking up in the estate category. Tommy and Jack wee surprised to get the estate of a local banker who had passed on, a couple of farmers, and several miners. They were busy and making a living.

Christmas was coming and Marion was excited about Santa Claus. Ann and Tommy took him to see the local Santa Claus, and he had his picture taken with him. When the Shinskis and O'Neils came over, he had to show them his picture with Santa.

Mary asked, "What did you ask Santa to bring you?"

Marion said, "A bear, a big bear."

Mary said, "I'm sure he will bring you a bear."

Mary O'Neil and Agnes Shinski were alternating Christmas dinners and this year they were all going to the Shinskis. When Christmas came, they all met at the Shinskis for dinner. Marion had two bears with him and was very happy.

Harry had his new wife with him. He and Mildred Osters had married just before Thanksgiving. The twins were still single, and Kay wasn't present since she was eating dinner at Harry Barnes's house.

After Mr. Shinski gave the prayer, they all ate and drank and visited. Ann and Tommy were the first ones to leave, as they wanted Marion to take a nap.

Tommy Victori, Samuel Rice, and Nick Linex, the three Democratic candidates, were to meet head to head at the Democratic Rally just before the primary election in March.

Tommy met with his boosters which now included two dozen people consisting of fourteen men and ten women. They had met periodically and covered the county well. They had collected three thousand dollars, which Tommy used in newspaper advertising and posters on signs all over the Limbo County area.

On the night of the rally, they had drawn lots and Samuel Rice was going to be the first speaker, Nick Linex was to go second, and Tommy felt fortunate to go last.

Samuel Rice talked about how he was going to be a tough prosecutor, and he would make it tough on the criminals so there would be less crime in Limbo County when he was elected.

Nick Linex almost repeated what Samuel Rice had said about making sure that all criminals would end up in jail. He would decrease the crimes in Limbo County when he was elected State's Attorney.

Tommy Victori said, "I have been an Assistant State's Attorney, and we have put criminals behind bars often and for long periods of time. I must add, however, that I will see that all gambling and hidden prostitution will, with the cooperation of the Sheriff's Office and the State Police, end in Limbo County."

The Democratic Primary vote was close, less than five hundred votes separated the three candidates. Tommy came out on top. At Democratic headquarters, Tommy, Mary, and Mike O'Neil, the twins, Paul and Jimmy, Kay, the Shinskis, the Wenzes, and all their friends celebrated Tommy's victory. Samuel Rice and Nick Linex came up and congratulated Tommy and promised him they would do all they could to help him win in November.

Tommy and Ann went home happy with their win. Tommy turned to Ann and said, "Now we have the big fight in the general election in November."

Ann said, "There seems to be no end to campaigning."

Tommy said, "We are due for a vacation. As soon as your school is out, we'll go somewhere."

Ann answered, "We'll count on that. Do you have any suggestions?"

Tommy said, "We went west to Colorado for our honeymoon and south to the Ozarks last June. What about going north to the Wisconsin Dells?"

Ann answered, "That sounds good to me."

Tommy said, "I'm all fagged out. Let's hit the sack."

The next day was just another day at the office for Tommy. He arrived at nine o'clock in the morning and was congratulated by Jack Wenz and their secretary. For Ann, it was another school day. She had coffee in the teacher's lounge and hurried to her first grade class. The children were already in their seats and cried out, "Good morning, Mrs. Victori."

Tommy sat down to plan his fall campaign. After a few weeks off, he would call a meeting of his campaign committee to see what could be done. He examined the financial report. He doubted that there was enough to pay the bills that would come due now that the primary election was over.

How would they be able to collect another three thousand dollars for the general election? He saw now why so many State's Attorneys and Sheriffs campaign committees accepted money from the red light district and gambling people. It made financing a campaign a lot easier. He knew, however, that he would not accept money from those he had promised to close. If they didn't have the three thousand dollars, they would settle for two thousand or even one if it became necessary.

Fifty-six

It seemed to come out of the blue, but the news was not unexpected. Mike O'Neil brought the news home. The John Sampson Coal Company was closing, shutting down for good, and like Hornby's, Old Clyde, and Gillespie's Old Den, Hinders was to be sealed and closed for good. The people would leave, seeking work in new coal mines. Hinders would become a ghost town. Lots, buildings, and houses would immediately drop to half the values that they had while the mine was operating and eventually be vacated and sold for a couple of hundred dollars to someone who was willing to tear down the structure for the wood.

All around Limbo County, central and southern Illinois mines were closing. The big Depression of the thirties was going full swing in 1934. Franklin D. Roosevelt, the new president, who had taken over Herbert Hoover's job was an optimist when he said, "We have nothing to fear, but fear itself." But he found that the world was in a depression and his efforts, which went by letter in capitals, CCC: Civilian Conservation Corporation, WPA: Works Progress Administration, and others, employed an average of two million workers over several years. They were helpful but were also increasing our national debt. They were a big help to the unemployed, but slow in helping the economy.

Mike O'Neil and Mary Victori-O'Neil decided that, for the present day, they would stay in Hinders. Their home and store were paid for. Mary decided that she would sell out her inventory and close the store. The taverns and the red light district were the first to go. Mike and Mary hoped that Harrick's, which operated a store and filling station, would stay open so those that continued to live in Hinders could buy their groceries and gasoline locally.

Mike O'Neil began to look for a new job immediately. His big hope was to get a job of some kind with the four Superior mines, which were already working shift work. The miners union voted to work three days a week, rather than fire forty percent of the workers when the conveyors went in the mines, and let attrition and those moving slowly cut the number of miners, and wait for the day when they would again be working five days a week.

The Roosevelt WPA, which gave jobs to the unemployed who worked in community services, taking care of streets, sidewalks, schools, post offices, state, county, and township roads and bridges, paid a person about forty-four dollars a month in small counties like Limbo and a little more in larger counties and cities.

These wages were supplemented with food stamps, used to buy the necessities of life at the grocery stores. There were soup kitchens and health care for the needy. There were people that had more, but the Great Depression made the large majority of people poor, so if you felt sorry for yourself all you had to do was look at your neighbors.

Mary met a disappointed Mike O'Neil each evening when he came home from job hunting. Fortunately, for the O'Neils, Mary had invested her savings and Mike's money in the United States Post Office, where their money was safe and they continued to receive an annual interest of two percent.

176

It was after the fourth of July before Tommy called his crew together again for his fall campaign for the general election. They were all in a good mood since Tommy won the Democratic Primary. Roosevelt and Horner, president and governor, were talking about running again in 1936, and their opposition was weak. They could not take things for granted, but they realized that Tommy Victori's Republican opponent, Francis Hooper, had a tough situation.

Tommy called the meeting to order and said, "It's a good thing that my opponent's party is having a rough time, but remember he had no opponent in the spring, so he spent very little money, and we spent all of ours. We were broke so I put one hundred dollars seed money in our treasury. "We'll try to collect some money, but I intend to run a campaign with as little advertising as possible.

"Are there any questions or suggestions?"

Mike O'Neil spoke up and said, "Tommy, as you know, I'm unemployed and I'll have plenty of time to go door to door to get you elected."

Tommy said, "Thank you, Mike, but I hope it won't be necessary."

Paul said, "We won't have as much time as Mike, but as brothers, Jimmy and I can work nights and weekends and throw some money into the campaign."

Jimmy said, "You can count on your twin brothers."

Tony Prima said, "Harry Shinski and I only work three days a week in the Superior Coal Company mines. We don't have any money, but we can join Mike O'Neil knocking on doors."

John Ford, the chairman of the group, said, "I've been waiting to see what others had to say. It should be a landslide, but nobody ever lost an election by getting

177

too many votes. I urge everyone to work like we did in the primary, when we all knew we had a tough election.

"Tony Prima, now that Tommy has won the primary and is the Democratic candidate, what are you hearing at the County meeting?"

Tony stood up and said, "The County Chairman and the Precinct Committeemen are all cautioning each other not to take the general election too lightly."

John Ford stood up again and asked, "Does anyone have any ideas for making money?"

Jimmy said, "Paul and I had planned on a dance and party at Hamburg's, but now that the Hinders mine has shut down, can anyone come up with a good location?"

John Ford said, "I think we should have a party to raise money at the county seat in Carmount, and I suggest the Elk's."

After a discussion, the group voted to have the dinner and dance on Saturday night on the second Saturday in September, providing they could get the Elk's club and a band.

John Ford said, "I'll take care of the Elk's club and band."

Tommy got up and gave John thanks and led in a round of applause. The meeting was adjourned after agreeing to meet again in three weeks.

Fifty-seven

Mike O'Neil came home and told Mary all about the meeting for Tommy's campaign for State's Attorney in the November election.

Mary said, "It sounds very good."

He replied, "The only real problem is a job for yours truly. I didn't tell you but I drove to Kollinson one day last week and checked at the Old Maggie Mine where I worked before coming back to Hinders. The place where I nearly lost a leg. They are laying off men. Mary, I know you do not want to move and neither do I, but if I don't get a job in driving distance by the first of the year, I'll be forced to go where jobs are available."

Mary replied, "I agree, but I pray every night that you get a job soon."

When the Hinders school had its registration before starting in September, there were only forty pupils, and the two new teachers, Miss Jones and Miss Pinta, knew that at the rate people were leaving Hinders now that the mine had shut down, it would be a one-room school next fall. They discussed their situation and decided they would both look for new teaching positions for the following year.

Jack Wenz and Tommy Victori were taken to Richard Rinso's lockbox by the man's son, David Rinso. The will had been made by an old lawyer who had since passed on. The two witnesses to the will were still working at the bank.

Richard Rinso had divided his assets equally between his son and daughter. The elder Rinso was the majority stock holder of the People's State Bank and owned a lot of other property in Gilmore. Although he had lost a good deal of money during the crash of the stock market in 1929, most of his money was in United States Government securities.

When the bank had been checked on March 6, 1933, the day Roosevelt declared a "Bank Holiday" and closed all banks in the United States until officials of the Department of the Treasury could examine every bank's book, the People's State Bank was among those in good financial condition and was supplied with money by the treasury and allowed to reopen.

Two other banks, national banks, were so badly in debt that they never reopened. That left the People's State Bank as the only bank in town and David Rinso and his sister, Donna Rinso, wealthy.

Jack Wenz and Tommy Victori were indeed fortunate to have the richest estate in Gilmore, which would take years to settle.

Fifty-eight

At the next meeting of Tommy Victori's boosters, Tommy thanked everyone for their help at the dinner/dance held in Carmount and said they cleared nine hundred twenty-two dollars.

Jack Wenz said, "As President of the Young Democrats, I want to say we have raised six hundred dollars, which we will spend for the entire Democratic ticket. That should give Tommy some help."

John Ford suggested that on the last two Saturdays before the election everyone should meet at the courthouse and divide into two groups, having a caravan go north and one go south one Saturday and then one go east and one go west the next Saturday; covering all the towns on the east and west of Limbo County. Planning in such a way that we would hit every village and town on the two Saturdays.

"We will give each caravan the towns to be covered north, south, east, and west when we meet at ten o'clock in the morning at the southside of the courthouse," said John Ford.

After some general discussion, the booster's club adjourned, satisfied that there would be a big Democratic victory to celebrate on the second Tuesday in November of 1934.

On the evening of the second Tuesday in November, Democrats and Republicans waited in the County Clerk's office and in the hallways and stairs for the returns to be posted. It was evident early that the Depression had kicked the Republicans with such a force that it would take years to recover.

Tommy and Ann, the O'Neils, the twins, Paul and Jimmy, Kay, and the Wenzes headed for the Democratic headquarters early as it was evident that it was a landslide for their party.

It was nearly midnight when Tommy and Ann finally left the celebration and headed home. Ann said, "Tommy, you are going to get your wish now. You will become State's Attorney of Limbo County."

Tommy answered, "I've given it a lot thought. Various State's Attorneys and Sheriffs have tried to close all gambling and prostitution in Limbo County and none have succeeded. I've got plans that I think will work."

Then Tommy added, with half a laugh, "I know one thing. I won't have to do anything about the redlight district in Hinders. The closing of the mine took care of that."

Ann agreed, "Fortunately for Maggie of the Black Cat, who was a good citizen in many ways, but got off on the wrong foot when she was young, she retired before the mine shut down."

Fifty-nine

Tommy and Jack discussed how the partnership would work when Tommy became State's Attorney in December. Since Limbo was a small county with a salary under ten thousand dollars, Tommy was permitted to continue to work in private practice. Jack suggested that they might be paid on the basis of the number of hours put in private practice. Tommy said, "That sounds like a good idea, but we can check it from time to time."

Jack said, "We want it flexible."

Tommy was in his office one day when an old friend dropped by. He immediately got up to shake hands with Wilbur Oster. Wilbur, a farmer adjoining Hinders, had gone through grade school and high school with Tommy. They graduated together from high school in 1924. Wilbur had taken over his father's farm when he graduated, and although Tommy had seen him occasionally, Wilbur had never discussed any legal business with him.

"Tommy, I want to congratulate you, our next State's Attorney."

Tommy answered, "Thank you, Wilbur. What can I do for you?"

Wilbur replied, "The bank has notified me that they are going to foreclose their mortgage on our farm."

"How big is the mortgage?" Tommy asked.

"It was originally ten thousand dollars, but we had paid half off. The last two years we have not been able to make the payments. As you know, corn only brings in twenty-five cents a bushel and hogs aren't much better.

The way things are in farming, we can't make our payments. We are hoping that the new subsidy program that Roosevelt has proposed will help out. However, we will need an extension of our mortgage to have a chance, and the bank has refused an extension."

"They are unreasonable in their demands," Tommy said.

Wilbur said, "Do you have any suggestions? I hate to see our farm lost after all the time and effort my father and I have put into it."

"There is a new farmer's loan program. Perhaps we can get some help," Tommy told Wilbur.

"I hope so," he replied.

Tommy said, "We can try. I'll check with the farm bureau and see what I can do. When is the closing date?"

"They have given me sixty days," Wilbur answered.

"Wilbur, you can count on me to try to help."

"Thanks, Tommy, I'll be back in a week. In the meantime, we are checking to see where we can move. It is a sad situation for farmers all over the United States."

Tommy said, "I'll get right on it."

Tommy checked with the Farmer's Home Administration. He then called Wilbur Oster and told him that he should have no trouble getting a five-thousand-dollar loan to pay off the bank. He made arrangements to go with Wilbur and follow the process, which was considered a small loan.

Sixty

Tommy was waiting for the first week in December when he would go to the courthouse to be sworn in with the rest of the county ticket, which included all the county officials elected with him, except the county superintendent of schools, who would be sworn in the first Monday in August.

The Victoris and the Shinskis were all present at the courthouse to congratulate Tommy. After the ceremony, the Democrats had a little party in the judge's quarters and all the new officers took their families and friends to visit their new offices.

The next day Tommy was in the State's Attorney's office early with his two assistants, a young lawyer named James Brown and an older lawyer named Henry Track. They looked over the criminal cases and paid special attention to a murder case which had gained headlines. A man on a date with a girlfriend had choked the young lady to death. The boyfriend had called up the Sheriff's Office and confessed. After he was arrested and brought to jail, he pleaded not guilty.

Tommy and his two assistants, none of whom were familiar with the case, made arrangements with the jailed man's lawyer, Earnest Batter, to see his client, Fred Hammer. When Earnest Batter came in, the three attorneys from the State's Attorney's office told Mr. Batter that they would give him half an hour with his client before they came over to the jail.

Mr. Batter said, "I'll be waiting."

When Tommy and his assistants got to jail, Mr. Batter said, "My client wants to plead not guilty."

"Is it alright if I ask him a question?" Tommy asked Mr. Batter.

Mr. Batter answered with, "Go ahead. As long as I'm here you can ask any question. I might tell my client not to answer it."

Tommy asked, "Mr. Hammer, were you out with Rita Lender on November twentieth, the night she died?"

"Yes, I was," Fred Hammer replied.

Tommy went on. "Did you call the Sheriff's Office and tell the Sheriff's Deputy that Miss Lender was dead?"

"Yes, I did. However, I did not kill her," Fred Hammer answered.

Tommy asked, "Can you tell us what happened?"

"I was out of gas, and I walked to the highway, went to the nearest station, got some gas, and when I got back, I found Rita Lender, strangled to death."

"Why did you say you killed her?"

Mr. Hammer said, "I was in such a state of shock that I felt to blame for her death that I said I killed her."

Tommy said, "Thank you, Mr. Hammer."

Tommy went back to his office with the two assistants and asked, "What do you think of Fred Hammer's story?"

Henry Track spoke up and said, "His story is not impossible, but difficult to believe. I checked through the file and he did go to a service station on the night in question."

James Brown said, "I checked the file, too, and he went for gas that night. However, I still believe that he has a lot of explaining to do."

"Do we let him out on bail?" Tommy asked.

His assistants answered, "No."

Tommy said, "I agree. We'll do research on the case."

Tommy and one of the Sheriff's detectives went to visit the service station where Fred Hammer went for gas the night that Rita Lender had died. He told the attendant that the time was important. The owner of the service station said, "We checked the time carefully. It was about ten o'clock in the evening."

Tommy said, "Mr. Hammer had called the Sheriff's Office about midnight. He had time to walk back to his car, find Miss Lender dead and drive to another tavern and phone in.

"When the coroner examined the body he thought she had only been dead three or four hours, but he couldn't be sure. If she had been killed before he went for gas, she would have been dead for a longer period."

The detective then drove Tommy to the tavern from which Fred Hammer had called the Sheriff's Office. The tavern owner confirmed the midnight hour.

Tommy went back and checked the file for Rita Lender, including the pictures taken. There was no doubt that she had put up a struggle, judging from her torn clothing. The hospital report indicated that she had been raped.

Tommy Victori presented all the evidence they had to Earnest Batter and said, "We are willing to listen to a plea."

Mr. Batter accepted the evidence and said nothing.

A couple of days later Earnest Batter came to see Tommy Victori and said, "I talked to my client several times. He is willing to plead murder in the second degree. It was not premeditated."

Tommy said, "We will listen to his plea and will consider murder in the second degree."

Sixty-one

Tommy, with the help of his assistants, was trying to determine where and when they would make their first raid. They decided that they would tackle gambling first. Of course, they knew that there were places in the county that had both gambling and prostitution, but they decided on gambling first.

The most gambling was going on in a small town called Dobson and its immediate vicinity. Tommy got together with the Sheriff and his deputies and decided to send men over a period of a week to check a place called Joe's and another called Homer's, and wait until a meeting, set to take place on the evening on the raid, to decide which one to hit.

Their observers had seen two craps tables and at least a dozen slot machines in each. The Friday night that Tommy selected they hit Homer's, at ten o'clock in the evening, and Joe's, at eleven o'clock, they found no gambling in either place. It was evident that Homer's and Joe's had been warned. Tommy's question was, "By whom?"

He and his two assistants met with Sheriff Joseph Anders, his Deputy Sheriff, and detectives trying to find the leak that tipped off Joe's and Homer's. Tommy asked Sheriff Anders to name the men that had spent several nights the last week as undercover investigators at Joe's and Homer's. The Sheriff pointed out two men that had visited Joe's and two men that had visited Homer's. The Sheriff did not name them, but that was not necessary as Tommy and his two assistants had interviewed the men before and after each visit.

"I have your report here. I'll read Joe's first. Last week, two of you went to Joe's on Monday, Tuesday, and Friday and saw gambling with two craps tables and ten slot machines. As you know, when we raided the place, we saw no gambling devices of any kind. What do you think happened?" asked Tommy.

They both threw up their hands and said in unison, "Somebody tipped them off."

Tommy turned to the two that visited Homer's. "You spent three evenings at Homer's and saw gambling at two craps tables and eleven slot machines. Is that right?"

"Yes," they both answered.

Tommy Victori turned to the group, "You know we are the laughingstock of Limbo County? Do any of you have any suggestions?"

Sheriff Joseph Anders spoke very loudly, "If I find out that there were any leaks in my department, the person or persons will be fired and prosecuted to the full extent of the law."

"There is only one way to solve this problem and that is to continue these raids until we break this gambling ring, and then we'll turn to the prostitution in this county. If I have to I'll turn to Governor Henry Horner and the State Police," Tommy said.

He waited two weeks while they brought men from the State Police who were unknown in Limbo County. These undercover police checked half a dozen places in the county. On the night and time, the Sheriff's men took a truck with them to the places selected by Tommy, and collected two craps tables and eight slot machines. The State Police took two trucks and raided another two places and brought three craps tables and twelve slot machines back to Carmount and stored them in the Sheriff's storeroom.

Tommy put an ad in the county papers asking the owners of the gambling equipment to claim the gambling equipment or it would be destroyed. He then waited thirty days and publicly had the equipment destroyed.

After three successful raids by the Sheriff and the State Police, the owners of the gambling taverns and prostitution interests realized that the new State's Attorney of Limbo County was going to be a tough man to deal with. They decided to have a meeting to see what could be done.

They met at one of the gambling taverns in Dobson. Big Joe, named for his six-foot five-inch frame, took charge. He told the large gathering, which included all the gambling and prostitution interests in Limbo County, "Every man has his price. I know that one way or another some of us let the State's Attorney know that we would have thousands of dollars ready for him and his campaign if he played ball. I also know that so far he has turned us down. I believe that every man has his price. We may have to raise fifty to one hundred thousand dollars to get this done, but we gotta do it. Does anyone have any suggestions?"

One of the men at the meeting said, "Where are we going to get that kind of money?"

Big Joe said, "I know it'll be tough, but we gotta do it if we are going to stay in business. I'll start by pledging ten thousand dollars. I don't have that kind of money, but I'll get it. Before we go any further, I want everyone in here to check the men around him. If there is anyone here we do not know, we will ask him to leave."

Big Joe gave the group five minutes. There were several that were in question until they were identified. Then Big Joe went on, "I'll appoint my bookkeeper to take down the pledges. He'll do this to get a total. When he gets the total, he'll announce it. There will be no names kept. He'll burn the papers before our eyes."

The pledges went on for an hour. The bookkeeper announced the total of seventy-five thousand dollars. Then he took out a match and nearly burned himself as he held the paper until it fell to the floor.

Big Joe said, "I know one of the Sheriff's deputies well enough to give him the message verbally."

The next week there was a notice in the Carmount paper that said:

> There are those in illegal gambling and prostitution interests that think the State's Attorney's Office is for sale. They are wrong. No amount of money will stop the raids on illegal gambling and prostitution in Limbo County.
> —Thomas Victori, State's Attorney of Limbo County.

Sixty-two

Tommy Victori began to get mail threatening his life and safety. The Sheriff assigned Tommy bodyguards twenty-four hours a day. Ann, Tommy's wife, and Mary Victori-O'Neil, his mother, became alarmed and did not hesitate to tell Tommy to ease up on the gamblers. Tommy told them he had no choice. He had the cooperation of the Governor and the Sheriff, and they must press on.

Tommy went to the State and County Liquor License Commission and had the liquor licenses of the three gambling places they raided suspended.

One evening when Tommy was getting out of his bodyguard's car, a shot rang out and a bullet grazed Tommy's head, leaving a scratch. Tommy was taken to Gilmore Hospital, treated, and brought home. Guards were posted around the Victori home. This was a big mistake by the gamblers because it turned the whole county against gambling and prostitution. Gambling and prostitution began to suffer where it really hurt; the money intake. Places that operated for years were closing. Tommy, the Sheriff, and the Governor kept the pressure on. More raids were made, more gambling equipment destroyed, prostitutes jailed and fined. Over a two-year period, Limbo County was over the hill. Illegal activities were crushed and moved out of the county.

The Victoris were so worried about the threats on Tommy's life that they did not announce that Ann was expecting their third child. Everyone except their immediate family and close friends were surprised to read in

192

the county newspapers that Ann had a girl who they named Mary Agnes in honor of her two grandmothers.

When Tommy and Ann brought Mary Agnes home, their first visitors were Mary Victori-O'Neil, her husband, Mike, Agnes Shinski, and her husband. The grandmothers were proud and happy with Mary Agnes, but they each brought a gift for Marion, who they knew would feel neglected. He had to be given a good deal of attention to make him happy about his new baby sister.

Aunt Kay also brought a present, having been warned by her mother not to forget about Marion and his inclusion on this happy occasion. The twins, Paul and Jimmy, also had presents for Marion and made it a point to spend time playing with him before they left.

Harry and his wife were also fans of Marion and held him while they were visiting the baby. However, in the next week, Marion wasn't sure he was happy to have a baby sister. He had been the center of attention since he was born, and now he had to share the attention with his sister. Ann and Tommy went out of their way to help Marion feel he was going to be Mary Agnes' helper and protector.

Kay, the last one in the Victori family, had graduated from the University of Illinois and was teaching at Springfield High School.

Mike O'Neil decided they would wait until spring, hoping he would find a job. He and Mary were so comfortable in their home in Hinders. They had closed off the store and lived in the rest of the house. Then too, with all the Victoris so near, he knew Mary would not be happy to leave.

Mike kept in close contact with the management of the Superior Coal Mines and they promised him that he would get on as a motorman. His wishes were partially realized when they notified him that they could use him three days a week as a motorman in mine number one, which was only three miles from Hinders. His first day on the job, he was met by Mary at the door with hugs and kisses. He laughed and said, "Mary, after being unemployed for months, it sure feels good to have a job again."

Mary had a working man's supper for him that evening, and they went to visit Tommy, Ann, Marion, and Mary Agnes. They were overjoyed that Mike and Mary would continue to live near them.

That evening Mike and Mary called the twins and Kay in Springfield and told them about Mike's new job and how happy they were.

The following weekend the twins came home with a surprise, two new girlfriends, twin sisters, Louise and Lucille. The girls were identical twins but it was not difficult to tell them apart after you got acquainted. Even Jimmy and Paul, who had looked so much alike during their first twenty years, were developing a little differently. All four of them were brunettes, with the males having skin a little darker.

Louise and Lucille worked for the State of Illinois for the Secretary of State. They had both graduated from the Springfield Junior College and had outgoing personalities. Paul and Jimmy had met them at a dance in Springfield and told them they had learned to dance at Hamburg's in Hinders. The twin sisters said they wanted to see the place so the Victori twins brought the sisters to the O'Neils. The Victoris then ended up at Hamburg's with the intention of leaving Hamburg's by eleven o'clock and driving back to Springfield in their 1935 V8 Ford.

Jimmy and Paul had so much fun introducing their girlfriends to their Hinders friends that the night went by quickly. However, they cornered their old friend, Mr. Hamburg, and asked him how business was going with the Hinders mine closed.

Mr. Hamburg said, "Better than I expected. We are still making a living and we pay in social security. It won't be much, but we will eventually retire. We don't intend to leave Hinders."

Jimmy and Paul were happy that Hamburg's was going to stay in Hinders. At eleven o'clock they danced the last dance of the evening with Louise and Lucille and headed for Springfield. It was after midnight when they stopped at the Springfield Diner for a bite to eat before they took the ladies home.

Kay enjoyed teaching shorthand, typing, and book-keeping at Springfield High School. Her Hinders, Gilmore High School, and University of Illinois boyfriend, who had majored in chemistry and physics, took a job teaching at Lanphier High School in Springfield. Thus, Harry Barnes and Kay Victori still spent a lot of time together. Kay roomed with a Springfield High School teacher in an apartment only a few blocks from her twin brothers, Paul and Jimmy.

All the Victoris, mother, daughter and three brothers, had paired off. Only Mary and Tommy were married, but the three others were serious about their companions.

Sixty-three

It wasn't long before Tommy Victori had his second murder case as State's Attorney. A farmer reported to the Sheriff's Office that his wife was missing.

Tommy and his assistant, Henry Track, drove to William Harvey's farm to talk to him. They decided not to phone ahead. When they arrived, William Harvey was with his uncle and aunt, Mr. and Mrs. Pete Harvey. William Harvey was in tears, emotionally distraught and mentally confused.

Tommy asked Mr. Harvey, "When was the last time you saw your wife?"

"I went to town this morning to buy some feed at the mill for my cattle. When I left, I told my wife, Martha, that I would be back in a couple of hours. When I got home, she was not at home. I wasn't alarmed because we have a couple of neighbors that she visits. When she did not come home for lunch, I called the two neighbors and they said she had not been there." At this point William Harvey broke down and his uncle and aunt put their arms around him, and tried to console him.

A couple of minutes later, he went on and said, "I called my uncle and aunt, Pete and Alice, who live only a couple of miles from me. When they arrived, they called my wife's father and mother who live in the Bloomington area. They weren't home. We finally contacted them and they are on their way here now."

Henry Track was talking to Pete Harvey and said to William, "I understand you have been married three years. Has anything like this happened before?"

The man answered, "We always have told each other when we were going to be gone any length of time."

Tommy and Henry decided to stay and wait for the arrival of Mr. and Mrs. John Subject, Martha Harvey's mother and dad, who arrived an hour later. Tommy and Henry asked permission to walk around the farm and came back to the house after the Subjects got there.

Tommy and Henry talked to Martha's parents and told them that their office and the Sheriff would do all they could to find Martha. Although everyone was worried, they believed that there had to be an explanation. Tommy Victori and Henry Track departed.

Two days went by, during which time they questioned every farmer within two miles of the Harvey farm. A couple of the closest neighbors said they had heard what sounded like gun shots coming from the Harvey farm late Friday afternoon. However, they said that was not unusual. William Harvey was a hunter and shot his shotgun in quail, rabbit, and squirrel season.

On Tuesday, Sheriff Joseph Anders came over to talk to Tommy and said, "We have done a lot of investigating. I'm beginning to think that William Harvey has something to do with his wife's disappearance."

He told Tommy about neighbors hearing shots on Friday about five o'clock in the evening. He also told Tommy that William Harvey did a lot of shooting during every hunting season. He said to Tommy, "I suggest that we have a private meeting with Mr. Harvey. Let's start at the farm this afternoon. I think we are going to have to use a little pressure."

Tommy said, "I believe you are right. Let's check to see if he is home, and if he is, let's go see him."

The Sheriff said, "I've got to get Mr. Harvey's permission to check the farm. He has no choice but to say yes.

Otherwise, I will have to proceeded with a search warrant."

William Harvey shook hands with Tommy Victori and Sheriff Joseph Anders. He seemed to have a little better control of himself although he looked red-eyed and exhausted from lack of sleep.

After they were seated, Tommy said, "I understand you have no leads about your wife's disappearance."

William Harvey answered, "None."

The Sheriff said, "I'll be frank with you, Mr. Harvey. Neighbors heard shots coming from your farm about five o'clock Friday evening. Are you sure that she was not shot by accident?"

Mr. Harvey answered immediately, "I'm sure." He did not become angry about the question.

The Sheriff said, "It's routine, but do we have your permission to search your grounds and dig anywhere on it?"

William Harvey jumped up and said, "You'll need a search warrant to do that."

Sheriff Joseph Anders said, "It'll look bad for you if you force us to get a search warrant."

William Harvey said angrily, "I'm going to call my lawyer."

Tommy Victori said, "Go call your lawyer. Tell him we want you and him to be in my office, the Office of the State's Attorney in Limbo County Courthouse, tomorrow at ten o'clock in the morning."

Tommy Victori and Joseph Anders thanked William Harvey and left.

The next day, Tommy and Joseph Anders met in the Office of the State's Attorney with William Harvey and his attorney, Jack Weber.

After the introductions, Jack Weber said, "I understand you all but accused my client of the murder of his wife."

Tommy answered and said, "We are following all leads and we want Mr. Harvey to explain if he was shooting his shotgun on his farm at about five o'clock on Friday evening."

Attorney Jack Weber said, "I'll tell my client if he should answer your question at this time."

Then he turned to his client and said, "Go ahead and answer the question."

William Harvey said, "I was shooting quail. I showed two of the quail I killed to my uncle and aunt, Mr. and Mrs. Pete Harvey. You can ask them."

The Sheriff asked, "Where was your wife?"

"At that hour, she was home preparing supper," Mr. Harvey said.

Tommy said, "We want to check all his land and house to see if we can find any clues to her disappearance."

"I think that can be arranged. Any other questions?" Jack Weber replied.

Tommy said, "We would like to start checking the land and house tomorrow."

Mr. Weber walked out with his client and said, "I'll be back in a few minutes."

When Mr. Weber came back, he said, "You can start checking the land tomorrow, but we would prefer that you wait until Friday to check the house."

Tommy and the Sheriff both said, "That will be fine."

The search parties found nothing related to the crime on Thursday or Friday. On Monday, the Sheriff's excavation crew found an area in a wooded section of the farm which seemed to be softer when stepped on than the neighboring ground. When they dug in the soft spot, they found a woman's body wrapped in two blankets. The body was identified as Mrs. William Harvey, maiden name Martha Subject.

When Tommy Victori and Sheriff Joseph Anders confronted William Harvey in the Limbo County Jail after he was arrested for the murder, he made a complete confession. William Harvey said he no longer loved his wife, Martha. He had another woman, and he asked his wife for a divorce. Because of her religion, Martha could not give him a divorce. William took her quail hunting, shot her, and then buried her in a wooded area of his land.

William Harvey appeared before the Circuit Judge of Limbo County. His confession was read to him, a confession which he signed. Judge Charles Marshall asked William Harvey to plead. William Harvey apologized to Martha's mother and father, relatives, and friends and said he was sorry and plead guilty. Judge Marshall set a date thirty days from then for sentencing.

When the date arrived the Judge asked witnesses who had reason to believe that William Harvey should not be sentenced to death to testify. William Harvey's father testified that his son had always been a good son, a good farmer, a community-minded citizen, breaking down while crying saying, "My son's life should be spared."

William Harvey's minister told how Mr. Harvey had gone to his church since he was a little boy, was a model in his behavior, always willing to help others and did not believe in capital punishment. The last one to testify was William Harvey's high school coach. He told what a good athlete William Harvey was in football and basketball. He said William was a team man and not the least bit selfish. He ended by saying that William Harvey's life should be spared.

Judge Charles Marshall announced a court recess for one half of an hour. At the end of the thirty-minute recess, the Judge read his decision sentencing William Harvey to death by hanging for the planned premeditated murder of his wife, Martha Harvey.

After the sentencing of William Harvey, Tommy went back to his office to finish some routine business. When he reached his house and went in he found Ann in the kitchen with Marion sitting on a kitchen chair near Mary Agnes who was lying down in her play pen and holding her own bottle and sucking happily.

He grabbed Marion, lifted him up and went over and hugged Ann with his free hand. Ann asked, "What sentence did the Judge give William Harvey?"

Tommy answered, "He went all the way, death by hanging."

"It is sad that things like this have to happen," Ann said.

Tommy agreed, "It is indeed sad for families, relatives, and friends."

Sixty-four

Things were going well for the Victori family clan. Time was moving so rapidly that Tommy was starting to plan for his second term as State's Attorney of Limbo County.

Some of the members of the Democratic party, Tommy's party, believed that Tommy Victori's closing the gambling and ending prostitution in Limbo County should entitle him to the nomination for Judge of the Seventh Judicial Circuit.

When they mentioned their plans to Tommy, he urged them to wait until he finished a second term as State's Attorney. He believed he would have no opponent from either party as State's Attorney.

He knew that for Judge of the Seventh Judicial Circuit, he would have a dogfight from the Republicans. There were six counties in the Seventh Judicial Circuit, with a population of over three hundred thousand people. In his mind, he named the six counties, starting with the largest, Sangamon, and the capital of Illinois, Springfield, and then naming them according to size: Macoupin, Morgan, Jersey, Green, and ending with the smallest, Scott.

Where would he get the money to run a six-county campaign? The more he thought about it, the more sure he was that he did not want the Democratic nomination for the Judge of the Seventh Judicial Circuit of Illinois, and as the caucus for the nomination approached, he told those in charge that he did not want the nomination at this time.

Just before the caucus, Jack Wenz, his law partner, came to him and said, "Tommy, the party wants you. You have no choice. The party is going to raise the money for your campaign. I'm going to nominate you at the caucus."

Tommy finally said, "Jack, go ahead, but remember, if I win, I'll no longer be able to practice law, and you'll need a new partner."

Jack said, "I don't want to lose you, but I'll be happy to see you kicked upstairs."

Tommy called his booster club together. He said, "Against my better judgment, I accepted the nomination of the Democratic caucus as Democratic candidate for Circuit Judge of the Seventh Judicial Circuit." Led by Mike O'Neil, everyone present applauded.

Tommy laughed and said, "Thank you. I've got to talk to the Democratic Chairman of each of the other five counties and see if we can get some help. Our next meeting will be in Sangamon, then Morgan, Jersey, Green, and finally Scott County. I don't see how candidates in Illinois do it. There is only one way, they get a lot of help from a lot of people and then collect a lot of money. I'm indeed fortunate to have the same booster's club I had in my campaign for Limbo County State's Attorney. I'm also very lucky that John Ford has agreed to again be my campaign chairman."

John Ford stood up and said, "It's going to take many meetings. Most of them will be in Sangamon County, which has more than half of the population of the Circuit. We won't ignore Limbo County, where Tommy is well known, but we'll save it for last."

While Tommy was campaigning for Judge, Ann was still teaching and taking care of Marion, who was six years old and in first grade, and Mary Agnes, who was two years old. She had the help of a babysitter and the grandmothers, Mary Victori-O'Neil and her mother, Mrs. Shinski.

Tommy was going out campaigning day and night. He did have one break in this campaign: the twins now engaged to the twin sisters, Louise and Lucille, and his sister, Kay, now engaged to Harry Barnes, all lived in Springfield and Sangamon County where he was doing most of his campaigning. Tommy was also fortunate that he had graduated from Illinois College in Jacksonville and Morgan County, and many of his former classmates of both parties agreed to help him get elected.

Finally, the second Tuesday in November came, and the election was over. Tommy Victori and Jack Wenz used their offices as a campaign headquarters. They had a number of phone lines and were connected with the County Clerks in the six counties, so they received the results as soon as they became available; Tommy Victori won all six counties, getting his greatest plurality in Limbo County.

Tommy and Ann, who had taken a week off from school, were exhausted but happy and thankful that the election had been so kind to the Victoris.

While Tommy Victori was waiting to be inaugurated, he went to Springfield to a clinic for new judges to learn procedures, do's and don'ts and the routine of being a judge. In the meantime, he was helping train Frank Jason, who was taking over his job as State's Attorney, and helping Jack Wenz and his new partner, Dean Basson, a young lawyer, become acquainted with all the cases and legal work he was leaving behind.

Tommy was sworn in as judge by his old friend, Francis Berging. All the O'Neils, the Victoris, the Shinskis, and his lifelong friends, Dean Basse, Louis Looke, Tony Prima, Mary Bruno, and Sally Sponick were present.

After the swearing in, they all went to the basement where Tommy had catering services so his family and friends and boosters could eat, drink, and visit. Tommy insisted on bringing Marion and Mary Agnes, who were in the care of their two grandmothers.

Sixty-five

The next week, Judge Tommy Victori had his first court case. It concerned two young men, just out of high school, who had no job or money. They broke into a grocery store and stole scores of cans of food, which they planned to sell on the black market.

They pleaded guilty and Judge Victori gave them advice about going to vocational school and getting some kind of training for a job when they came out of prison. Judge Victori gave the two young men his first sentence; sixty days in the Vandalia Prison, since this was their first offense.

The second case was a date rape case. Tommy had read the preliminary hearing and set a date for the case to be tried. He selected a date in early January of 1939. He checked with the prosecutor and the defendant's lawyer, and they both approved the date.

Before the date for the date rape case, set by Judge Victori, arrived, the new State's Attorney, Frank Jason, came over to see Tommy Victori and said, "I'm dropping the date rape case against the defendant, Nick Lucas."

Tommy Victori looked at Frank Jason and asked, "What happened?"

Frank Jason grinned and answered, "The young lass who brought the case asked me to drop it."

Tommy Victori said, "She what?"

"She accepted an engagement ring and is going to marry Nick Lucas," Frank Jason said.

Tommy Victori laughed and said, "I had your job as State's Attorney for four years, and I had a lot of surprises, too."

The next two cases for Judge Victori were domestic violence cases. The first was the Jones case. Nellie Jones was the mother of three children, two boys who were ten and twelve years old and a girl who was fourteen. The mother had put up with an abusive husband for years. When she learned from her daughter that the girl's father, her husband, had tried, over a period of several months, to get in bed with their daughter, who had been too afraid to tell her, she knew that divorce was the only answer.

When Mrs. Jones heard this, she waited until her husband had gone to work, packed her clothes and her children's clothes and drove to her parents' home fifty miles away. She left him a note telling him she had put up with his abusive behavior for years, but when Jennie, their daughter, told her that her father had tried on numerous occasions to get in bed with her, she decided that all there was left was a divorce.

Her husband drove to her parents' home and tried to persuade her to come home. When she refused, he threatened her and said that he was going to court to get the children.

Judge Victori had the child custody case. The husband, whom Mrs. Jones was divorcing, did not appear in court. Judge Victori awarded custody of the children to the mother.

The second domestic case involved an abusive husband who had been ordered by the court to stay away from his wife and two children, twin girls who were twelve years old. When Tommy got the case, the husband,

Andrew Johnson, had been arrested for continually following his wife, who was seeking a divorce.

Judge Victori read the court restraining order to him and asked, "Mr. Johnson, do you understand what this court order says?"

"Yes, but I want to see my children," Mr. Johnson replied.

Judge Victori sentenced him to a week in jail and continued the restraining order when he got out of jail. Then he told Mr. Johnson, "If you obey the restraining order thirty days after you get out of jail, we'll have a hearing and make arrangements for you to see your daughters in a supervised situation."

Mr. Johnson, then, was taken back to jail.

Sixty-six

After Tommy was sworn in as Circuit Judge, the twins called their mother, Mary Victori-O'Neil, and told her that they wanted to come to Hinders on Sunday with their girlfriends. They had an announcement they wanted her to put in the paper.

Mary laughed and said, "You want to announce the date of your marriage?"

Paul on one phone and Jimmy on another phone booth said, "How did you guess that, Mom?" Then all of them laughed.

Paul said, "We'll be at your house in an hour, Mom, because we are all ready to jump into one of our 1935 V8 Fords."

Jimmy said, "We had one 1935 V8 Ford between us, and since we will soon be living in different locations, we bought a second 1935 V8 Ford."

Paul added, "And they both look alike, too, Mom."

When the two sets of twins arrived, Mary and Mike were waiting for them. All anyone could hear was congratulations and each said how happy he or she was.

Jimmy said, "We made it easy for you, Mom; Louise Rosel and Lucille Rosel and Paul and I sat down and we wrote down the announcement we would like to have in the paper."

Mary and Mike read it. Mary said, "This is a standard wedding announcement. The only thing that makes it different is it involves you four."

Mike spoke up and said, "It is different; two sets of twins do not get married very often."

Mrs. Victor Rosel phoned Mary Victori-O'Neil and was all excited about planning the wedding at the Springfield Cathedral.

The two women met in Springfield to plan the wedding of the Victori twin brothers to the Rosel twin sisters.

Mrs. Rosel and her daughters selected the wedding gowns for the two brides, the two maids of honor, and the four bridesmaids. The brides would be in traditional white, and the other gowns were to be in royal blue.

The wedding was to take place on the first Saturday in June.

The reception was to be in the Knights of Columbus Hall in Springfield, where the dinner and dance were to be held.

The first Saturday in June finally arrived. All the Victoris and Rosels were excited, and that included Marion who at seven was to be the ring bearer, and Mary Agnes, who at three was the flower girl. All the men were dressed in black tuxedos, with Tommy Victori and Harry Shinski as best men.

When the wedding march was played by the organist, the brides' father, Joseph Rosel, came down the aisle with his daughter Lucille on his left arm and his daughter Louise on his right arm. Many of the guests gasped and smiled their pleasure. Few had ever seen the beautiful scene of a father marching twin brides down the aisle to marry twin brothers.

The wedding reception, dinner and dance were enjoyed by the Victoris, Rosels, and their guests. After the dance, the twins separated, Jimmy and Lucille headed for a honeymoon at Niagara Falls, and Paul and Louise going to the mountains of Denver, Colorado for their honeymoon.

Kay Victori and Harry Barnes were married the first Saturday in August in 1939. Tommy Victori gave away his beautiful sister, dressed in a floor-length white wedding gown.

Harry Barnes and Kay Victori, who had gone together from Hinders grade school through Gilmore High School and the University of Illinois, exchanged wedding vows in the Gilmore Catholic Church. The reception dinner and dance were held at the Gilmore County Club, where all the Victoris learned to golf.

The Barnes, Victori, and O'Neil families and friends enjoyed the evening. The relationship of the group, most of whom had grown up together, was so intimate that everyone would cherish the memory of this happy occasion.

After the last dance, the smiles, the handshakes, and good-byes, the newlyweds departed for the honeymoon to Florida and the islands.

Sixty-seven

Judge Tommy Victori, a former teacher, was approached by the Sangamon County Superintendent of Schools about taking on the task of being an arbitrator in a dispute between the Springfield Board of Education and the Springfield Education Association. The teachers were talking about going on strike.

Tommy Victori told the County Superintendent, "I'll be glad to try to help prevent a strike, if both sides are willing to have me as an arbitrator."

Judge Tommy Victori received a written invitation from the teachers and the Board of Education to be the arbitrator of the disagreement. He had both sides file a brief describing the problem, explaining their point of view, and telling why they felt they were right in their position.

After studying the annual financial reports of the district for the last three years, Tommy found that money was the problem. The teachers and the Board of Education both agreed that money was the problem. There had been nearly a decade of Depression years. The state was the major source of funding for most Illinois schools, and because of the big Depression had not been able to give the school district the necessary funding.

The same big Depression had cut down the values of the home, farms, businesses, factories, plants, and other property, thus the assessed valuations, salaries, wages, and incomes had gone down giving the schools less money locally. The schools had cut teachers, administrators, and other personnel and closed schools and made classes larger. The teachers were doing more work without increases in pay. This had gone on for several years.

They all agreed that a state income tax had to be instituted in Illinois. This could only be done by the legislature and the Governor. In the meantime, the schools had no choice but to borrow money and operate as frugally as possible.

Tommy, after listening to both sides, and taking time to ponder the problem, suggested that the teachers and other personnel be given a small salary increase and that the Springfield School District, through their state teacher's organizations, and the Board of Education, through its state organizations, work with the legislature and Governor to institute an income tax in Illinois.

The Board of Education, at an executive session, decided to give the teachers a raise of two hundred dollars for the year. This was then done in an open meeting. The teachers at an evening meeting accepted the Board of Education's offer and agreed to work to begin an income tax in Illinois.

Sixty-eight

On September 1, 1939, Germany bombed and invaded Poland. Germany took Poland, Denmark, Luxembourg, the Netherlands, Belgium, Norway, Yugoslavia, France, and Greece. Germany and the Axis had active allies in Italy, Hungary, Romania, and Bulgaria.

Then Germany bombed and attacked Britain. When Germany was unable to get Britain to surrender, it attacked Russia. The United States of America instituted selective service in 1940. The Victori twins, Jimmy and Paul, registered for the draft. Harry Barnes, Kay Victori's husband, also registered. Everyone waited excitedly for the draft numbers to be drawn.

Jimmy, Paul, and Harry all had numbers above two thousand. Jimmy and Paul realized that unless something unforeseen happened, they and Harry would not be called the first year of the draft. Therefore, Jimmy and Paul could continue working as civil engineers for the Department of Transportation, and Harry could continue in his job as chemistry and physics teacher at Lanphier High School. They could all continue living with their wives in Springfield, Illinois.

On December, 7, 1941, Japan bombed Pearl Harbor in Hawaii, and the United States Congress declared war on Japan. We were now in World War II. Germany and Japan and Axis were fighting the Allies, led by the United States and Britain.

In 1943, the twins, Jimmy and Paul, volunteered for the army engineering corps, and were commissioned Second Lieutenants. At the end of the 1943 school year, Harry Barnes volunteered for the navy.

Mary Victori-O'Neil was present with their wives, Louise and Lucille, to bid good-bye to Jimmy and Paul, the sons and husbands who departed to go into the officer training in the army. Mary Victori-O'Neil was also present with her daughter, Kay, bidding good-bye to her husband, Harry Barnes, when he departed for basic training in the navy. Each time Mary came home, she expressed her sorrow for the wives of her sons and the sadness for her daughter to Mike O'Neil.

The war changed the entire economy of the nation. The Superior Coal Mines began to work six days a week, with Mike O'Neil working all six. The factories and war industries needed workers with over twelve million men and women going into the service.

The United States became the arsenal of democracy. When the war started we had twenty-five hundred war planes and seven hundred sixty war ships. When the war ended, we had eighty thousand war planes and twenty-five hundred war ships.

The second good-bye for the twins and Harry Barnes came when they finished training and went back to be shipped out. Jimmy and Paul were shipped to England to help prepare for the landing on France on D-Day. The Axis knew it was coming and the Allies knew it. Such a big undertaking would take probably years of preparation. The brain force of the Generals and all their command would decide when and where.

Mary Victori-O'Neil and the twins' wives received regular correspondence from Jimmy and Paul. When the twins wrote their mother a letter about their troop ship, to England, it brought back memories to Mary of her trip to the United States with Marion when they traveled third-class.

The troop ship was guarded against German submarines by destroyers and cruisers, which made the twins' troop ship as safe as possible. The troop ship had hundreds of soldiers that slept on anchored bed frames covered with canvas. It was real close quarters, and many of the soldiers became seasick and, like Mary and Marion, vomited overboard.

When Harry Barnes got back to Navy Pier on Lake Michigan in Chicago, his company received orders to be shipped to the Pacific Coast in forty-eight hours, which meant that he would leave Chicago early Wednesday morning. On Tuesday evening, at ten o'clock, as he was lying in his bunk, a member of the shore patrol came to his barracks. Harry thought he must have been dreaming. He heard the night duty officer asking Harry Barnes to report to the barracks office. Harry thought, *My gosh, there must be someone ill at home.* His thoughts, immediately, turned to his wife, Kay.

He hurried to the office, not forgetting to salute the officer on duty. He saluted and said, "Mr. Barnes the commanding officer wants to see you."

The man from the shore patrol said, "Mr. Barnes, follow me."

Harry went to a waiting shore patrol car and was taken to headquarters. By then, Harry was becoming nervous. However, he did not forget to salute the commanding officer.

After his salute was returned, the commanding officer said, "At ease."

Harry relaxed a little. The commanding officer said, "The Naval Academy Preparatory School at Bainbridge, Maryland needs a physics teacher. In checking our records, we found that you were teaching high school physics at Lanphier High School in Springfield, Illinois. Is that correct?"

Harry answered, "That is correct, sir."

"I've already called Bainbridge and they have given their approval for you to teach physics there."

Harry said, "Thank you, sir, but my company is shipping out in the morning."

The commander looked at Harry and said, "We'll take care of that. You'll head to Bainbridge, Maryland for your new assignment in the morning."

A surprised Harry said, "Thank you, sir."

When Harry Barnes arrived at Bainbridge, he was taken to the commanding officer of the Naval Academy Preparatory School. He saluted the commanding officer who returned the salute.

He told Harry to be seated. He then proceeded to tell Harry about the school. "We have about one thousand students. They are young men from the regular navy, Marines, and coast guard who want to enter Annapolis and become commissioned officers. We felt that they would be better prepared for Annapolis if we gave them preparatory courses in algebra, geometry, trigonometry, and an introduction to calculus, chemistry and physics." He paused and then said, "That's where you come in, biological science, English, and American History and any other course we think necessary. There is a lot of competition because only three hundred who make the best test scores of the one thousand enter the Academy each year."

He looked at Harry and asked, "Any questions?"

Harry asked, "What classification will I have?"

The commander said, "All teachers are commissioned officers. You will undergo an officer training course and be commissioned an Ensign."

Harry, who had been writing his wife, Kay, regularly decided that this welcome news needed a phone call. He was then taken by an Ensign to the physics department, to the head of the department, who was a full Lieutenant as a commissioned officer. After he met a half a dozen teachers in the physics department, he was taken for a tour of the school grounds.

Harry thought before the navy took over this stately high school, it must have been an exclusive school for the children of people with money. Then he went back to the physics department and was given a copy of the physics book that was being used, a study guide and a set of tests that had been given. He was assigned a mentor who had many suggestions about teaching at the Naval Academy Preparatory School.

The school operated on a strictly military basis. When a teacher entered a classroom, a student hollered "Attention" and all the students stood up until the teacher said, "At ease." The students obeyed the rules or were sent back to the regular service.

Harry Barnes knew his subject well and how to teach it. His students learned to listen carefully. When the tests were given, Harry's students tested well above the average.

The staff at the Naval Academy Preparatory School at Bainbridge, Maryland knew that the school year ended on June 10, 1944. They knew that the three hundred students who made the best grades on the tests would go to Annapolis after a vacation. They also knew that the other students would return to the regular service in the navy, Marines, and coast guard.

The question was, what would the teaching staff do during the summer? The announcement came from the Commander at a faculty meeting the first week in June. The faculty, except the heads of each department who would stay at Bainbridge and plan for the next school year of 1944–1945, would depart for Camp Perry, Virginia on June 15th for a two month assignment as teachers in the navy literacy program.

The army had been taking the illiterates, who enlisted or were drafted, sending them through a literacy program for one year, and those who learned to read and write to a certain standard were placed in the regular army. Those that did not meet the required standard were given an honorable discharge. The navy had agreed to participate in the literacy program and established the program at Camp Perry, Virginia.

The Commander said, when the faculty returned in the middle of August, approximately one half of them would be assigned to William and Mary College in Williamsburg, Virginia, where a second Naval Academy Preparatory School would start. However, they would all return to Bainbridge, Maryland before being assigned to William and Mary.

Harry Barnes had never been to Virginia. When the train taking the Naval Academy Preparatory School teachers south crossed the Virginia border, the black passengers got up and headed for the back of the train. When Harry and his friends visited Williamsburg, they saw drinking fountains marked white and black, toilets marked black and white, black and white churches, black and white eateries, and other places that were segregated, including schools. Harry had seen a lot of prejudice in the North but had not realized how complete segregation was in the South.

The teachers were assigned to temporary barracks because they would only be in Camp Perry for two months. Since they were commissioned officers, they had their own eating quarters.

The next day, after breakfast, they were told that they would be helping the teaching staff in the literacy program in Camp Perry. The program consisted primarily of teaching navy recruits how to read and write. Many of the men knew arithmetic and were especially good at counting money. However, there were classes in arithmetic.

Harry Barnes was assigned a teacher. The teacher, Mrs. Jackson, was a civilian primary teacher who had been recruited by the navy from a public school. He was introduced to Mrs. Jackson, who introduced him to the class as Ensign Harry Barnes, a teacher in the Naval Academy Preparatory School in Bainbridge, Maryland who came here to help in the summer program.

Mrs. Jackson told Harry, "I want you to observe the first week." Then she handed him a notebook and added, "Take all the notes you want, but be sure to observe and study our procedures which will help you when you take over the class."

Harry looked askance at Mrs. Jackson.

She smiled and said, "You'll get your chance."

Harry looked over the class of fifteen men. Mrs. Jackson said, "The navy wants these men to learn to read and write as quickly as possible. You'll find them eager to learn; they want to write home to their sweethearts, wives, mothers, and fathers as soon as possible."

Harry took notes. He was concerned. How would he teach these navy men to read and write? He watched and listened to Mrs. Jackson. She used the phonetic method to teach letters and words. He smiled as he realized that that was the method used by his teachers to teach him and his classmates.

Harry Barnes had been taught to write by the Palmer method. Mrs. Jackson used the Palmer method plus a tracing procedure. The navy student would put tracing paper above the words and trace the letters and words.

In a few weeks, they would trace over standard letters to their wives, mothers, and fathers. The students learned to read the words. They had the biggest smiles on their faces as they enclosed the letters in an addressed stamped envelope. As time went by, they learned to address their own letters.

On the second day of the second week, after talking to Ensign Harry Barnes, Mrs. Jackson said to the class, "Ensign Harry Barnes is going to teach this class for the next hour."

Harry smiled and said, "I have taught high school students for a number of years. My field is chemistry and physics. I've watched and listened to Mrs. Jackson for over a week, and I have been fortunate in having such a good mentor to learn from."

Harry Barnes then went on with the lesson plan for the day, pronouncing words phonetically and doing his best to help the students. It took Ensign Harry Barnes a couple of weeks of handling individuals, groups, and the entire class before he could relax completely.

Harry wrote long letters to his wife, Kay, and phoned her often, telling her of his teaching in the literacy program at Camp Perry, Virginia.

When the temporary duty at the literacy program in Camp Perry, Virginia was over, the staff of the Naval Academy Preparatory School returned to Bainbridge, Maryland. Two weeks later, Harry Barnes and nearly one half of the teaching faculty were assigned to William and Mary College in Williamsburg, Virginia to start a second branch of the Naval Academy Preparatory School.

Sixty-nine

The Americans, British and Canadians assembled three million men, five thousand large ships, four thousand smaller landing crafts, and more than eleven thousand aircraft for the D-Day invasion. Before the invasion, Allied bombers pounded the Normandy Coast to prevent the Germans from building up their military strength.

The invasion had been set for June 5th, 1944, but storms forced the Allies to postpone it one day until June 6th, 1944, D-Day. The world had never seen an invasion of this magnitude. Paratroopers went ahead to cut railroad lines, blow up bridges, and seize landing fields.

Jimmy and Paul were never as afraid in their lives as when they and other engineers were crossing from England to France in a landing craft. As far as their eyes could see in either direction and in front of them and behind them, they saw landing crafts. The noise of guns firing from shore and ships was beyond human ears and minds to comprehend.

When the landing craft came near shore, Jimmy and Paul followed the others in the craft and waded to shore. The horror of men falling and dying all around them was unbelievable. How Jimmy and Paul reached the beach safely, they would never know.

Male nurses and medical corps men were trying to take care of the injured and dying. The landing Allies pressed on, climbing over walls and trenches.

It took the Allies several days to secure a beachhead and bring in big guns and equipment. At times, the Allies were stalled but never stopped for long.

When they reached streams and rivers, if a bridge had been blown up, the engineers and their men would wait until the waterway was secure, and then they used pontoons, flat-bottomed boats, to build temporary bridges.

Jimmy and Paul Victori, all the Americans, and all the Allies were treated well by the French. The French appreciated the fact that the hated Germans were retreating before the Allies and France would again be free.

When French towns were liberated, the French could not do enough for the Allies. The French were destitute. The Americans supplied them with food, and it seemed that all Frenchmen drank and smoked. The Americans had plenty of cigarettes, and the French had plenty of wine hidden away in their cellars.

When Jimmy and Paul had weekend liberty, they could always drink and smoke and have a good time. The soldiers who were interested had young French women ready to take care of them.

Jimmy and Paul would never forget their first weekend in Paris after the Germans departed from the city. They, along with other soldier friends, had a French dinner at one of the many French restaurants. Then, it was girly-show time. They went to a burlesque show. They listened to the singing and watched the dancing. There was a lot of low comedy and a striptease show. The soldiers went wild. Some of them went up on the stage and hugged and kissed the women.

Houses of prostitution were all over Paris. Before the soldiers went on liberty they were shown movies of men in various stages of suffering from venereal diseases, such as syphilis and gonorrhea, transmitted chiefly by sexual intercourse. The pictures included penises that were covered by horrible-looking sores and pus formation. After the movie, a Sergeant, Lieutenant or Captain would give a lecture and say, "Regardless of what you see in the movies and what we tell you, we are realistic and know that man being man, many of you and that includes married men that have wives at home, will engage in sexual intercourse. Therefore, even if you have no intention of having sexual intercourse, take rubbers, condoms, with you. The army wants to protect all of you, so if you engage in sexual intercourse, even if you use a condom, there are prophylactic stations in Paris and here at the base. Stop in and be treated. That way you'll have double protection." Paul watched Jimmy procure a package of condoms. He followed and also got a package. Then, they looked at each other and laughed.

Jimmy and Paul learned as the Allies fought their way through France and Germany what men in battles found confronting them. Civilians get up in the morning, go to the bathroom, have breakfast, kiss their wives and children good-bye, go to work where there are toilet facilities, have lunch where there are toilet facilities, go home where there are bathroom facilities, have supper, help the children with their homework, etc., have a bed to sleep in with bathroom facilities, and are not in danger from the enemy.

In enemy territory, a soldier is always in danger of being shot from close-range, enemy guns at long distance, planes, or friendly fire. A soldier carries his own toilet paper and water. Then when he is moving when nature calls he has to look for a place to urinate or have a bowel movement. A soldier fights in all kinds of weather: hot, cold, rainy. Sometimes he burns up; other times he freezes.

Then there are extreme circumstances like D-Day when there is no rest and a soldier goes on fighting hour after hour and day after day, when men are injured and killed all around him as he is attacking and pushing forward.

Then there is the other extreme, as in the Battle of the Bulge when on January 16, 1944, thirty-eight mechanized German divisions, under the cover of fog followed by snow and extreme cold, attacked along a fifty-mile front near the Rhine River. Soldiers stayed and fought and fought and died and died. Thousands on each side were injured, and thousands on each side were killed.

The Allies crossed France and rushed toward the heart of Germany. Russian armies rolled toward Berlin from the east. From all directions, Allied armies closed in on Germany.

From the invasion of France on June 6, 1944, the Germans finally surrendered on May 8, 1945, V-E Day, Victory in Europe. The Allies were turning their attention to Japan and were planning on invading Japan.

The millions of soldiers in Germany had had enough fighting, but they were bravely waiting for orders to take part in crossing oceans to get to the Far East when the United States dropped atomic bombs on August 6, 1945 on Hiroshima and then on Nagasaki three days later. These atomic bombs made an invasion of Japan unnecessary. The Japanese surrendered marking the end of World War II on board the U.S.S. *Missouri* in Tokyo Bay on September 2, 1945.

Historians find it difficult to measure the costs of World War II. They can only estimate. World War II took the lives of more persons than any war in history. The guestimate of civilians and military dead totals fifty-five million. An estimate of casualties cannot be given with any accuracy.

The United States lost over four hundred thousand men and women and suffered over a million casualties. Man's inhumanity to man should have been a lesson, but since World War II ended, wars have continued, continued, and continued.

When the twins, Jimmy and Paul came home from England and were discharged from the army, they came home to Gilmore on the Illinois Terminal Railroad. At the station waiting for them were their wives, Louise and Lucille, and their mother, Mary Victori-O'Neil, and Mike O'Neil, Judge Tommy Victori, Ann, Marion, Mary Agnes, Kay, and Harry Barnes. The welcoming was enthusiastic and joyful with a lot of hugging and kissing.

Then Tommy told the twins, "We are going to Hinders where all the Victoris grew up and finish this celebration in the store where Mom made us a living and managed to save money to send all four Victoris to college."

They all got into the automobiles and headed for Hinders, the starting place of *Let Us Live* and the ending place of *Life Goes On.*